# MYSTIFYING

## SINISTER STORIES
### OF THE UNEXPLAINED

**KINGFISHER**

First published as *Mystery Stories* 1996 by Kingfisher
This edition first published 2008 by Kingfisher
an imprint of Macmillan Children's Books
a division of Macmillan Publishers Limited
20 New Wharf Road, London N1 9RR
Basingstoke and Oxford
Associated companies throughout the world
www.panmacmillan.com

ISBN: 978-0-7534-1632-7

1 3 5 7 9 10 8 6 4 2
1TR/0508/PROSP/(MA)/80NP/C

A CIP catalogue record for this book is available from the British Library.

Printed in China

# MYSTIFYING

# SINISTER STORIES OF THE UNEXPLAINED

CHOSEN BY
## HELEN CRESSWELL

KINGFISHER

# CONTENTS

# THE GREEN ARCHES
## JOAN AIKEN

THERE WERE THREE things needed before the charm would work. Rather like making a cake, when you want eggs, flour, sugar: it had to be raining, the day had to be Friday, and I had to have had the Dream the night before.

So, on Thursday nights, I would do everything I possibly could to bring on the Dream – look at pictures in picture-books of doors, arches, trees and forests, I'd sit and think and try to remember all the different times I'd had the Dream. Sometimes it worked, sometimes not.

The Dream chooses its own time to visit me. And, when I wake, I don't always remember; but I know when it has touched me, because I feel very calm when I wake, and things work out well for me that day.

I do still have the Dream, which is a comfort.

Oh, there's a fourth thing I forgot to mention, the most important of all. My brother Bran had to be singing his song.

The words of the song go like this:

*When we say goodbye*
*And wonder why*

# MYSTIFYING

*It has to be*
*And shall we never see*
*Each other's face again*
*What can I say?*

*I think that love and pain*
*Will never die*
*But last for evermore*
*I think that they*
*Carry us like the sea*
*On to a farther shore.*

My brother Bran made up the words, and he made up the tune too. It is a very simple tune, there are only seven notes in it, really, and when you hear it the first time you think that you will easily be able to remember it. The seven notes chase each other round and round in what my brother calls a *fugue*. And, while he sings the words to this tune, he will be playing a trickly, wandering jingle on his guitar, so it is like a bridge covered with vines. You can see the shape of the bridge, and you can see the vines as well. But, afterwards, you can never remember it. *Never*.

My brother Bran plays the clarinet, piano, guitar and mouth-organ. Or he did, before old Mrs Busby next door began to get so angry with us.

I'll come to her in a minute.

First I'll tell you about what happens when my brother plays and sings his song.

# THE GREEN ARCHES

The start of it all was when I was about six. I was sitting under our kitchen table, playing with a conker and a piece of string. And the music suddenly came into Bran's head, and he sang it. As he played and sang, I found that I wasn't under the table, but outside in the street. Standing up.

Castle Street, where we live, winds uphill in a curve. All the houses on our side are shaped like pieces of pie, wider in front than at the back. Between the houses run narrow alleys, closed off from the street by wooden doors. The paths are very narrow, and the doors are always shut. People don't use them much. Some of the doors I've never even seen open. I used to make up tales about what was behind them – mountains, deserts, palaces.

Well. First, like I say, I was listening to Bran's music, then – suddenly – I was outside Mrs Busby's door beside her house. I walked quickly to the door – I could walk – and lifted the latch. The door opened; and I was inside. The narrow mossy path led straight ahead into a wood. And what a wood! The trees, tall as pylons, had branches that curved up and met like the stone arches in the roof of a church; you couldn't tell where one tree ended and the next began.

My brother Bran's tune carried me forward through the glade – easily, quickly – as if I were a woodpecker, rising and falling. I knew that I was going to the very heart and centre of the wood, and that I would find something marvellous there.

But I didn't get there. The music stopped. And – in the flick of an eyelash – there I was back sitting under the kitchen table with my string and my horse-chestnut.

"Play that again, Bran!" I begged him, and he did. But – as I soon found – it never works more than once on the same day. And it has to be Friday, and it has to be raining, and I have to have had the Dream the night before.

But Mrs Busby, next door, seemed to hate us more and more. She began complaining about Bran's music and saying she couldn't stand all that row. That was after our dad got a job installing alarm systems in people's houses. The first one he installed – to try it out – was in our own house. And Bran came home from school, not knowing the number you have to tap out on the little keyboard, quickly, as soon as you step through the front door. So the alarm went off. I will say that's just about the loudest noise you can think of. You're afraid it's going to lift the teeth right out of your gums. Or the roof off the house. And, while Bran was running round looking for the bit of paper with the numbers written on it, all Mrs Busby's bees, from the hive in her back garden, rose up in a huge black spiral, like a tornado, and left for ever. They never came back.

So you can see why she had bad feelings against us; though it wasn't exactly our fault, and of course Dad apologized, and offered to replace the bees. But she said no to that, she had her own bee supplier. He brings them in a black van at night. Some people say she's a witch. She's certainly very bad-tempered.

I always looked forward to Fridays, when Bran came home for the weekend, for then he'd play his tune and then – sometimes, but not always – I'd float off to the wood. Sometimes it needed the tune and words both, sometimes only the tune.

Every time, I hoped I'd get to the centre of the wood, and, every time, the music stopped just before that happened.

"If only you'd written the tune just a bit longer!" I said to Bran. "If only there were nine notes instead of seven!"

But, he said, tunes make themselves, like plants growing, you have to take them as they come.

Still, I visited that wood so many times in the next year or two that I felt it belonged to me, and I was sure that, somehow, one day, I'd find my way to the middle.

Time went by. I started at school. Dad took me there in his delivery van.

And Mrs Busby got nastier. The second lot of bees weren't, she said, as good as the ones that had gone. And then she said Bran had got to stop playing his music in our house, for her nerves couldn't stand it. So, after that, Bran had to go off to his friend Ostin Morgan's house. The Morgans live outside the town, where there are no neighbours to complain.

"It's a bit hard on Huw," Bran said to our Dad. "He misses the music."

*Misses!* I felt as if someone had sucked away the air I needed for breathing. Before, Bran had played all through the weekend. And Mrs Busby used to rap angrily on the wall.

Dad said, "We have to live with our neighbours. They've got rights too."

So, what Bran started doing was, he'd play his harmonica as he rode down the street on his bike. When he got close to our house he'd play the tune of *When We Say Goodbye*, quite loud, so that I could hear it through our front window.

And – sometimes – that was enough to start me off. Like a leaf in a gale, I floated through Mrs Busby's door and off to the wood.

Birds sing in that wood, and bees hum; there are flowers, primroses, growing at the foot of the trees, and the bees float over them. Their hum is like the wind in telegraph wires. Sometimes I wondered if those were the bees that our alarm signal had driven away from Mrs Busby's garden.

(We never use the alarm system; but Dad says he likes the little red and green eyes, winking, so friendly and welcoming, in the corners of rooms.)

But – will you believe it – even Bran, just riding along on his bike in the street, playing his harmonica, even that was enough to put Mrs Busby in a rage.

"She's got acid instead of blood in her veins," said Dad.

"Poor thing. I pity her, really," said Mam.

And one day, as Bran rode past, playing the tune – and I was just beginning to float off, halfway from our kitchen to the wooden door – Mrs Busby opened her upstairs window and chucked a jugful of water all over Bran.

Perhaps she just wanted to give him a wetting, but it turned out more serious. The cold water in his face made him swerve, right into the way of a big truck that was coming down the hill. The truck braked and skidded into Mrs Busby's gate. And all its load – nineteen tons of frozen chip potatoes – crashed over the gate into the path beside her house.

And my brother Bran and his bike were somewhere under

all that frozen, heavy load.

They got him out, after a while. And he was taken away to hospital and put in intensive care. Unconscious he was, see, and no way could they find to rouse him. All that music trapped inside, and no door by which it could come out.

"I'm afraid I can't hold out much hope," the chief doctor told Dad, after three weeks had gone by.

They'd only let me go to see him once. There he lay, flat on a bed, with tubes feeding into him, and tubes leading out; he looked more like an alarm system than a person. Ostin Morgan's sister Angie wheeled me there in my chair, but when she saw Bran she burst out crying – she and Bran had been good friends – and we had to leave again. I wondered if the tune was running round and round inside Bran's head, the notes chasing each other like raindrops. As we left, I tried to send a message to him: "Bran! Think of the tune. Remember the tune. It might help you." But I got no answer at all.

The truck driver had not been badly hurt, but the company who owned the truck and the nineteen tons of frozen chips were very angry with Mrs Busby; and she was just as angry with them. For it seemed that she had been keeping her new lot of bees in their hives just inside the wooden door, on the path at the side of her house, and the frozen load had fallen on them and finished them off. So the truck owners were going to law, and Mrs Busby was going to law.

"You are the ones who have really suffered," Mrs Morgan said to my mam. "With your poor boy hanging like that between life and death, and the little fellow already handicapped the way he is. You are the ones who should be going to law."

"What good would law do us?" says Mam. "Law can't make our boys better."

I had a feeling that, if only Bran's tune could be played for him – if only he could hear it – that might undo some knot or latch that would open a way for him to the world again. *If only I could remember the tune*, I thought. But that tune is like my Dream – every time, it slips away before you can grab it.

Mrs Morgan surprised me, though.

"My husband has a plan," she said.

Mr Morgan is Bran's music teacher.

"He has written down a song that your son wrote," she told Mam. "And it's going to be played on Radio Camelot next Friday. And Tom's going to get the doctor's permission to take a transistor into the ward and play it, just in case Bran might be able to hear it."

Mam shook her head doubtfully . . . "*Nothing* reaches him," she said.

I was sitting in my wheelchair in a corner of the kitchen. And I thought two things. One: *when they play it on the radio I shall be able to visit my wood again. But only if I have the Dream the night before. Oh, please, please let me have the Dream!*

And the other thought: *if only I could get to the middle of the wood, perhaps I could find something there, perhaps I could bring something back, that would help Bran, that would set him free. Bring him home.*

I asked Mam, I begged and pleaded to be allowed to go to

the hospital when Mr Morgan went in with his transistor, to play the tune. But I was not allowed.

"You can listen to it at home, in the kitchen," said Dad. "Angie Morgan is coming in to sit with you."

It rained, that Friday. It *poured*. Bad weather for bees. They stay at home, in their snug hives.

I'd had the Dream the night before, so I was hopeful. As usual, I could not remember what it had been about, but I could feel the afterglow from it.

At three, Angie switched on the transistor.

"Radio Camelot," said the voice. "Here is a pot-pourri from the hills and the valleys. First, a beautiful song written by a teenage boy, sung by the famous tenor Robin Price." Robin Price, I knew, was a friend of Mr Morgan. He sang Bran's song very well, and calmly. No sooner had the first three notes floated from the box than I was away, going through Mrs Busby's entrance, along her path, into my wood. Right to the heart of it.

And what did I find there?

I found my brother Bran, under the green arches, filled with peace and light.

"This is the place to be, Huw," he says to me. "This is the best place. No wonder you were always trying to come back. But it's not your turn just yet. Your turn will come though; don't you fret."

Next – to my utter amazement – I saw Mrs Busby. But she was much smaller. She seemed like a child, looking about her as if she'd been struck dumb with wonder. Staring up at the great green arches above, down at the bees floating among the primroses.

"I didn't know," she kept murmuring. "I didn't know it was like this. And – just next door, all the time!"

Then Bran's tune ended and, with a breaking heart, I was snatched away, back to my own life, my own kitchen. Angie was in oceans of tears, with her head on the table, and the phone was ringing.

I wheeled myself over and answered it.

"I'm afraid it's sad news," said my dad's voice. "Bran did hear the tune. He opened his eyes and smiled at us all. And then he took and died."

Well.

I was sad as could be; and yet I could have been sadder, for I was sure, inside me, where Bran had got to, and I couldn't be sorry for that.

It's a comfort to know where he is. Some day I shall join him, and sometimes, when they play his tune on the radio, I have a chance to get a glimpse of him. If I've had the Dream the night before, that is, and it's a rainy Friday.

Here's a queer thing.

After Dad had rung off, Angie and I looked out of the window. And we saw the sky black, as if a dust storm had blown into our town.

But it wasn't a dust storm. It was bees. All Mrs Busby's first lot had come back, to take up residence in their hives again. But it was too late for Mrs Busby. She, it was found, had died of a heart attack, just about the time they were playing Bran's song on the radio.

She'd got no kin, we heard. She was all alone in the world. Poor woman. So Dad took over her bees. They live in our back yard now, furry, friendly things, and the humming they make is like harp music. I look after them – it's a thing I can do well, in my wheelchair – and I tell them all that happens.

Sometimes I tell them bits of my Dream, if I remember enough.

It's about coming home, you could say.

# THE AZTECK OPAL
## RODRIGUES OTTOLENGUI

"MR MITCHEL," BEGAN Mr Barnes, the detective, after exchanging greetings, "I have called to see you upon a subject which I am sure will enlist your keenest interest, for several reasons. It relates to a magnificent jewel; it concerns your intimate friends; and it is a problem requiring the most analytical qualities of the mind in its solution."

"Ah! Then you have solved it?" asked Mr Mitchel.

"I think so. You shall judge. I have today been called in to investigate one of the most singular cases that has fallen in my way. It is one in which the usual detective methods would be utterly valueless. The facts were presented to me, and the solution of the mystery could only be reached by analytical deduction."

"That is to say, by using your brains?"

"Precisely! Now, you have admitted that you consider yourself more expert in this direction than the ordinary detective. I wish to place you for once in the position of a detective, and then see you prove your ability.

"Early this morning I was summoned, by a messenger, to go aboard the steam yacht *Idler*, which lay at anchor in the lower bay."

"Why, the *Idler* belongs to my friend Mortimer Gray," exclaimed Mr Mitchel.

"Yes!" replied Mr Barnes. "I told you that your friends are interested. I went immediately with the man who had come to my office, and in due season I was aboard the yacht. Mr Gray received me very politely, and took me to his private room adjoining the cabin. Here he explained to me that he had been off on a cruise for a few weeks, and was approaching the harbour last night, when, in accordance with his plans, a sumptuous dinner was served, as a sort of farewell feast, the party expecting to separate today."

"What guests were on the yacht?"

"I will tell you everything in order, as the facts were presented to me. Mr Gray enumerated the party as follows. Besides himself and his wife, there were his wife's sister, Mrs Eugene Cortlandt, and her husband, a Wall Street broker. Also, Mr Arthur Livingstone, and his sister, and a Mr Dennett Moore, a young man supposed to be devoting himself to Miss Livingstone."

"That makes seven persons, three of whom are women. I ought to say, Mr Barnes, that, though Mr Gray is a club friend, I am not personally acquainted with his wife, nor with the others. So I have no advantage over you."

"I will come at once to the curious incident which made my presence desirable. According to Mr Gray's story, the dinner had proceeded as far as the roast, when suddenly there was a slight shock as the yacht touched, and at the same time the lamps spluttered and then went out, leaving the room totally dark. A second later the vessel righted herself and sped on, so that before any panic ensued, it was evident to all that the danger had passed. The gentlemen begged the ladies to resume their seats, and remain quiet until the lamps were lighted; this, however, the attendants were unable to do, and they were ordered to bring fresh lamps. Thus there was almost total darkness for several minutes."

"During which, I presume, the person who planned the affair readily consummated his design?"

"So you think that the whole series of events was prearranged? Be that as it may, something did happen in that dark room. The women had started from their seats when the yacht touched, and when they groped their way back in the darkness some of them found the wrong places, as was seen when the fresh lamps were brought. This was considered a good joke, and there was some laughter, which was suddenly checked by an exclamation from Mr Gray, who quickly asked his wife, 'Where is your opal?'"

"Her opal?" asked Mr Mitchel, in tones which showed that his greatest interest was now aroused. "Do you mean, Mr Barnes, that she was wearing the Azteck opal?"

"Oh! You know the gem?"

"I know nearly all gems of great value; but what of this one?"

"Mrs Gray and her sister, Mrs Cortlandt, had both donned décolleté costumes for this occasion, and Mrs Gray had worn this opal as a pendant to a thin gold chain which hung round her neck. At Mr Gray's question, all looked towards his wife, and it was noted that the clasp was open, and the opal missing. Of course it was supposed that it had merely fallen to the floor, and a search was immediately instituted. But the opal could not be found."

"That is certainly a very significant fact," said Mr Mitchel. "But was the search thorough?"

"I should say extremely thorough, when we consider it was not conducted by a detective, who is supposed to be an expert in such matters. Mr Gray described to me what was done, and he seems to have taken every precaution. He sent the attendants out of the salon, and he and his guests systematically examined every part of the room."

"Except the place where the opal really was concealed, you mean."

"With that exception, of course, since they did not find the jewel. Not satisfied with this search by lamplight, Mr Gray locked the salon, so that no one could enter it during the night, and another investigation was made in the morning."

"The pockets of the seven persons present were not examined, I presume?"

"No! I asked Mr Gray why this had been omitted, and he said that it was an indignity which he could not possibly show to a guest. As you have asked this question, Mr Mitchel, it is only fair for me to tell you that when I spoke to Mr Gray on the subject he seemed very much confused. Nevertheless, however unwilling he may have been to search those of his guests who are innocent, he emphatically told me that if I had reasonable proof that any one present had purloined the opal, he wished that individual to be treated as any other thief, without regard to sex or social position."

"One can scarcely blame him, because that opal was worth a fabulous sum. I have myself offered Gray twenty-five thousand dollars for it, which was refused. This opal is one of the eyes of an Azteck Idol, and if the other could be found, the two would be as interesting as any jewels in the world."

"That is the story which I was asked to unravel," continued Mr Barnes, "and I must now relate to you what steps I have taken towards that end. It appears that, because of the loss of the jewel, no person has left the yacht, although no restraint was placed upon anyone by Mr Gray. All knew, however, that he had sent for a detective, and it was natural that no one should offer to go until formally dismissed by the host. My plan, then, was to have a private interview with each of the seven persons who had been present at the dinner."

"Then you exempted the attendants from your suspicions?"

"I did. There was but one way by which one of the servants could have stolen the opal, and this was prevented by Mr Gray. It was possible that the opal had fallen on the floor, and, though not found at night, a servant might have discovered and have appropriated it on the following morning, had he been able to enter the salon. But Mr Gray had locked the doors. No servant, however bold, would have been able to take the opal from the lady's neck."

"I think your reasoning is good, and we will confine ourselves to the original seven."

"After my interview with Mr Gray, I asked to have Mrs Gray sent in to me. She came in, and at once I noted that she placed herself on the defensive. Women frequently adopt that manner with a detective. Her story was very brief. The main point was that she was aware of the theft before the lamps were relighted. In fact, she felt someone's arms steal around her neck, and knew when the opal was taken. I asked why she had made no outcry, and whether she suspected any special person. To these questions she replied that she supposed it was merely a joke perpetrated in the darkness, and therefore had made no resistance. She would not name anyone as suspected by her, but she was willing to tell me that the arms were bare, as she detected when they touched her neck. I must say here, that although Miss Livingstone's dress was not cut low in the neck, it was, practically, sleeveless; and Mrs Cortlandt's dress had no sleeves at all. One other significant statement made by this lady was that her husband had mentioned to her your offer of twenty-five thousand dollars for the opal, and had urged her to permit him to sell it, but she had refused."

"So! It was Madam that would not sell. The plot thickens!"

"You will observe, of course, the point about the naked arms of the thief. I therefore sent for Mrs Cortlandt next. She had a curious story to tell. Unlike her sister, she was quite willing to express her suspicions. Indeed, she plainly intimated that she supposed that Mr Gray himself had taken the jewel. I will endeavour to repeat her words:

"'Mr Barnes,' said she, 'the affair is very simple. Gray is a miserable old skinflint. A Mr Mitchel, a crank who collects gems, offered to buy that opal, and he has been bothering my sister for it ever since. When the lamps went out, he took the opportunity to steal it. I do not think this, I know it. How? Well, on account of the confusion and darkness, I sat in my sister's seat when I returned to the table. This explains his mistake, but he put his arms round my neck, and deliberately felt for the opal. I did not understand his purpose at the time, but now it is very evident.'

"'Yes, madam,' said I, 'but how do you know it was Mr Gray?'

"'Why, I grabbed his hand, and before he could pull it away I felt the large cameo ring on his little finger. Oh! there is no doubt whatever.'

"I asked her whether Mr Gray had his sleeves rolled up, and though she could not understand the purport of the question, she said, 'No'. Next I had Miss Livingstone come in. She is a slight, tremulous young lady, who cries at the slightest provocation. During the interview, brief as it was, it was only by the greatest diplomacy that I avoided a scene of hysterics. She tried very hard to convince me that she knew absolutely nothing. She had not left her seat during the disturbance; of that she was sure. So how could she know anything about it? I asked her to name the one whom she thought might have taken the opal, and at this her agitation reached such a climax that I was obliged to let her go."

"You gained very little from her, I should say."

"In a case of this kind, Mr Mitchel, where the criminal is surely one of a very few persons, we cannot fail to gain something from each person's story. A significant feature here was that though Miss Livingstone assures us that she did not leave her seat, she was sitting in a different place when the lamps were lighted again."

"That might mean anything or nothing."

"Exactly! but we are not deducing values yet. Mr Dennett Moore came to me next, and he is a straightforward, honest man if I ever saw one. He declared that the whole affair was a great mystery to him, and that, while ordinarily he would not care anything about it, he could not but be somewhat interested because he thought that one of the ladies, he would not say which one, suspected him. Mr Livingstone also impressed me favourably in spite of the fact that he did not remove his cigarette from his mouth throughout the whole of my interview with him. He declined to name the person suspected by him, though he admitted that he could do so. He made this significant remark:

"'You are a detective of experience, Mr Barnes, and ought to be able to decide which man amongst us could place his arms around Mrs Gray's neck without causing her to cry out. But if your imagination fails you, suppose you enquire into the financial standing of all of us, and see which one would be most likely to profit by thieving? Ask Mr Cortlandt.'"

"Evidently Mr Livingstone knows more than he tells."

"Yet he told enough for one to guess his suspicions, and to understand the delicacy which prompted him to say no more. He, however, gave me a good point upon which to question Mr Cortlandt. When I asked that gentleman if any of the men happened to be in pecuniary difficulties, he became grave at once. I will give you his answer.

"'Mr Livingstone and Mr Moore are both exceedingly wealthy men, and I am a millionaire, in very satisfactory business circumstances at present. But I am very sorry to say, that though our host, Mr Gray, is also a distinctly rich man, he has met with some reverses recently, and I can conceive that ready money would be useful to him. But for all that, it is preposterous to believe what your question evidently indicates. None of the persons in this party is a thief, and least of all could we suspect Mr Gray. I am sure that if he wished his wife's opal, she would give it to him cheerily. No, Mr Barnes, the opal is in some crack, or crevice, which we have overlooked. It is lost, not stolen.'

"That ended the interviews with the several persons present, but I made one or two other enquiries, from which I elicited at least two significant facts. First, it was Mr Gray himself who had indicated the course by which the yacht was steered last night, and which ran her over a sand bar. Second, someone had nearly emptied the oil from the lamps, so that they would have burned out in a short time, even though the yacht had not touched."

"These, then, are your facts? And from these you have solved the problem? Well, Mr Barnes, who stole the opal?"

"Mr Mitchel, I have told you all I know, but I wish you to work out a solution before I reveal my own opinion."

"I have already done so, Mr Barnes. Here! I will write my suspicion on a bit of paper. So! Now tell me yours, and you shall know mine afterwards."

"Why, to my mind it is very simple. Mr Gray, failing to obtain the opal from his wife by fair means, resorted to a trick. He removed the oil from the lamps, and charted out a course for his yacht which would take her over a sand bar, and when the opportune moment came he stole the jewel. His actions since then have been merely to cover his crime, by shrouding the affair with mystery. By insisting upon a thorough search, and even sending for a detective, he makes it impossible for those who were present to accuse him hereafter. Undoubtedly Mr Cortlandt's opinion will be the one generally adopted. Now what do you think?"

"I think I will go with you at once, and board the yacht *Idler*."

"But you have not told me whom you suspect," said Mr Barnes, somewhat irritated.

"Oh! That's immaterial," said Mr Mitchel, calmly preparing for the street. "I do not suspect Mr Gray, so if you are correct you will have shown better ability than I. Come! Let us hurry!"

On their way to the dock, from which they were to take the little steam launch which was waiting to carry the detective back to the yacht, Mr Barnes asked Mr Mitchel the following questions:

"Mr Mitchel," said he, "you will note that Mrs Cortlandt alluded to you as a 'crank who collects gems'. I must admit that I have myself harboured a great curiosity as to your reasons for purchasing jewels, which are valued beyond a mere conservative commercial price. Would you mind explaining why you began your collection?"

"I seldom explain my motives to others, especially when they relate to my more important pursuits in life. But in view of all that has passed between us, I think your curiosity justifiable, and I will gratify it. To begin with, I am a very wealthy man. I inherited great riches, and I have made a fortune myself. Have you any conception of the difficulties which harass a man of means?"

"Perhaps not in minute detail, though I can guess that the lot of the rich is not as free from care as the pauper thinks it is."

"The point is this: the difficulty with a poor man is to get rich, while with the rich man the greatest trouble is to prevent the increase of his wealth. Some men, of course, make no effort in that direction, and those men are a menace to society. My own idea of the proper use of a fortune is to manage it for the benefit of others, as well as one's self, and especially to prevent its increase."

"And is it so difficult to do this? Cannot money be spent without limit?"

"Yes; but unlimited evil follows such a course. This is sufficient to indicate to you that I am ever in search of a legitimate means of spending my income, provided that I may do good thereby. If I can do this, and at the same time afford myself pleasure, I claim that I am making the best use of my money. Now I happen to be so constructed, that the most interesting studies to me are social problems, and of these I am most entertained with the causes and environments of crime.

Such a problem as the one you brought to me today is of immense attractiveness to me, because the environment is one which is commonly supposed to preclude rather than to invite crime. Yet we have seen that despite the wealth of all concerned, someone has stooped to the commonest of crimes – theft."

"But what has this to do with your collection of jewels?"

"Everything! Jewels – especially those of great magnitude – seem to be a special cause of crime. A hundred-carat diamond will tempt a man to theft, as surely as the false beacon on a rocky shore entices the mariner to wreck and ruin. All the great jewels of the world have murder and crime woven into their histories. My attention was first called to this by accidentally overhearing a plot in a ballroom to rob the lady of the house of a large ruby which she wore on her breast. I went to her, taking the privilege of an intimate friend, and told her enough to persuade her to sell the stone to me. I fastened it into my scarf, and then sought the presence of the plotters, allowing them to see what had occurred. No words passed between us, but by my act I prevented a crime that night."

"Then am I to understand that you buy jewels with that end in view?"

"After that night I conceived this idea. If all the great jewels in the world could be collected together, and put in a place of safety, hundreds of crimes would be prevented, even before they had been conceived. Moreover, the search for, and acquirement of these jewels would necessarily afford me abundant opportunity for studying the crimes which are perpetrated in order to gain possession of them. Thus you understand more thoroughly why I am anxious to pursue this problem of the Azteck opal."

Several hours later Mr Mitchel and Mr Barnes were sitting at a quiet table in the corner of the dining-room at Mr Mitchel's club. On board the yacht Mr Mitchel had acted rather mysteriously. He had been closeted a while with Mr Gray, after which he had had an interview with two or three of the others. Then when Mr Barnes had begun to feel neglected, and tired of waiting alone on deck, Mr Mitchel had come towards him, arm-in-arm with Mr Gray, and the latter said, "I am very much obliged to you, Mr Barnes, for your services in this affair, and I trust the enclosed cheque will remunerate you for your trouble."

Mr Barnes, not quite comprehending it all, had attempted to protest, but Mr Mitchel had taken him by the arm, and hurried him off. In the cab which bore them to the club the detective asked for an explanation, but Mr Mitchel only replied, "I am too hungry to talk now. We will have dinner first."

The dinner was over at last, and nuts and coffee were before them, when Mr Mitchel took a small parcel from his pocket, and handed it to Mr Barnes, saying, "It is a beauty, is it not?"

Mr Barnes removed the tissue paper, and a large opal fell on the tablecloth, where it sparkled with a thousand colours under the electric lamps.

"Do you mean that this is —" cried the detective.

"The Azteck opal, and the finest harlequin I ever saw," interrupted Mr Mitchel. "But you wish to know how it came into my possession? Principally so that it may join the collection and cease to be a temptation to this world of wickedness."

"Then Mr Gray did not steal it?" asked Barnes, with a touch of chagrin in his voice.

"No, Mr Barnes! Mr Gray did not steal it. But you are not to consider yourself very much at fault. Mr Gray tried to steal it, only he failed. That was not your fault, of course. You read his actions aright, but you did not give enough weight to the stories of the others."

"What important point did I omit from my calculation?"

"I might mention the bare arms which Mrs Gray said she felt round her neck. It was evidently Mr Gray who looked for the opal on the neck of his sister-in-law, but as he did not bare his arms, he would not have done so later."

"Do you mean that Miss Livingstone was the thief?"

"No! Miss Livingstone being hysterical, she changed her seat without realizing it, but that does not make her a thief. Her excitement when with you was due to her suspicions, which, by the way, were correct. But let us return for a moment to the bare arms. That was the clue from which I worked. It was evident to me that the thief was a man, and it was equally plain that in the hurry of the few moments of darkness, no man would have rolled up his sleeves, risking the return of the attendants with lamps, and the consequent discovery of himself in such a singular disarrangement of costume."

"How do you account for the bare arms?"

"The lady did not tell the truth, that is all. The arms which encircled her neck were not bare. Neither were they unknown to her. She told you that lie to shield the thief. She also told you that her husband wished to sell the Azteck opal to me, but that she had refused. Thus she deftly led you to suspect him. Now, if she wished to shield the thief, yet was willing to accuse her husband, it followed that the husband was not the thief."

"Very well reasoned, Mr Mitchel. I see now where you are tending, but I shall not get ahead of your story."

"So much I had deduced, before we went on board the yacht. When I found myself alone with Gray I candidly told him of your suspicions, and your reasons for harbouring them. He was very much disturbed, and pleadingly asked me what I thought. As frankly I told him that I believed that he had tried to take the opal from his wife – we can scarcely call it stealing since the law does not – but that I believed he had failed. He then confessed; admitted emptying the lamps, but denied running the boat on the sand bar. But he assured me that he had not reached his wife's chair when the lamps were brought in. He was, therefore, much astonished at missing the gem. I promised him to find the jewel upon condition that he would sell it to me. To this he most willingly acceded."

"But how could you be sure that you would recover the opal?"

"Partly by my knowledge of human nature, and partly because of my inherent faith in my own abilities. I sent for Mrs Gray, and noted her attitude of defence, which, however, only satisfied me the more that I was right in my suspicions. I began by asking her if she knew the origin of the superstition that an opal brings bad luck to its owner. She did not, of course, comprehend my tactics, but she added that she 'had heard the stupid superstition, but took no interest in such nonsense'. I then gravely explained to her that the opal is the engagement stone of the Orient. The lover gives it to his sweetheart, and the belief is that should she deceive him even in the most trifling manner, the opal will lose its brilliancy and become cloudy. I then suddenly asked her if she had ever noted a change in her opal. 'What do you mean to insinuate?' she cried out angrily. 'I mean,' said I, sternly, 'that if an opal has changed colour in accordance with the superstition this one should have done so. I mean that though your husband greatly needs the money which I have offered him you have refused to allow him to sell it, and yet you have permitted another to take it from you tonight. By this act you might have seriously injured if not ruined Mr Gray. Why have you done it?"'

"How did she receive it?" asked Mr Barnes, admiring the ingenuity of Mr Mitchel.

"She began to sob, and between her tears she admitted that the opal had been taken by the man I suspected, but she earnestly declared that she had harboured no idea of injuring her husband. Indeed, she was so agitated in speaking upon this point, that I believe that Gray never thoroughly explained to her why he wished to sell the gem. She urged me to recover the opal if possible, and purchase it, so that her husband might be relieved from his pecuniary embarrassment. I then sent for the thief, Mrs Gray told me his name; but would you not like to hear how I picked him out before we went aboard? I still have that bit of paper upon which I wrote his name, in confirmation of what I say."

"Of course, I know now that you mean Mr Livingstone, but would like to hear your reasons for suspecting him."

"From your account Miss Livingstone suspected someone, and this caused her to be so agitated that she was unaware of the fact that she had changed her seat. Women are shrewd in these affairs, and I was confident that the girl had good reason for her conduct. It was evident that the person in her mind was either her brother or her sweetheart. I decided between these two men from your account of your interviews with them. Moore impressed you as being honest, and he told you that one of the ladies suspected him. In this he was mistaken, but his speaking to you of it was not the act of a thief. Mr Livingstone, on the other hand, tried to throw suspicion upon Mr Gray."

"Of course that was sound reasoning after you had concluded that Mrs Gray was lying. Now tell me how you recovered the jewel?"

"That was easier than I expected. I simply told Mr Livingstone when I got him alone, what I knew, and asked him to hand me the opal. With a perfectly imperturbable manner, understanding that I promised secrecy, he quietly took it from his pocket and gave it to me, saying, "'Woman are very poor conspirators. They are too weak.'"

"What story did you tell Mr Gray?"

"Oh, he would not be likely to enquire too closely into

what I should tell him. My cheque was what he most cared for. I told him nothing definitely, but I inferred that his wife had secreted the gem during the darkness, that he might not ask her for it again; and that she had intended to find it again at a future time, just as he had meant to pawn it and then pretend to recover it from the thief by offering a reward."

"One more question. Why did Mr Livingstone steal it?"

"Ah! The truth about that is another mystery worth probing, and one which I shall make it my business to unravel. I will venture two prophecies. First – Mr Livingstone did not steal it at all. Mrs Gray simply handed it to him in the darkness. There must have been some powerful motive to lead her to such an act; something which she was weighing, and decided impulsively. This brings me to the second point. Livingstone used the word conspirator, which is a clue. You will recall what I told you that this gem is one of a pair of opals, and that with the other, the two would be as interesting as any jewels in the world. I am confident now that Mr Livingstone knows where that other opal is, and that he has been urging Mrs Gray to give or lend him hers, as a means of obtaining the other. If she hoped to do this, it would be easy to understand why she refused to permit the sale of the one she had. This, of course, is guesswork, but I'll promise that if anyone ever owns both it shall be your humble servant, Leroy Mitchel, Jewel Collector."

# WUTHERING HEIGHTS
## EMILY BRONTË

*Mr Lockwood, who has just taken over the tenancy of
Thrushcross Grange, is already aware of mysteries and secrets.
He rides over to Wuthering Heights to meet his landlord, Mr
Heathcliff, and finds a grim and cheerless household. He is
aghast when during his visit heavy snow starts to fall, and he
is forced to spend the night there. He is taken to his room,
where he discovers some mildewed books belonging to
Catherine Earnshaw. The window ledge is scratched with
names: Catherine Earnshaw . . . Catherine Heathcliff . . .
Catherine Linton . . . At last he falls into an uneasy sleep,
filled with strange dreams in which he is being attacked.*

THIS TIME, I remembered I was lying in the oak closet, and
I heard distinctly the gusty wind, and the driving of the snow;
I heard, also, the fir-bough repeat its teasing sound, and
ascribed it to the right cause: but it annoyed me so much, that
I resolved to silence it, if possible; and, I thought, I rose and
endeavoured to unhasp the casement. The hook was soldered
into the staple: a circumstance observed by me when awake,
but forgotten. "I must stop it, nevertheless!" I muttered,

knocking my knuckles through the glass, and stretching an arm out to seize the importunate branch; instead of which, my fingers closed on the fingers of a little ice-cold hand! The intense horror of nightmare came over me: I tried to draw back my arm, but the hand clung to it, and a most melancholy voice sobbed, "Let me in – let me in!" "Who are you?" I asked, struggling, meanwhile, to disengage myself. "Catherine Linton," it replied shiveringly (why did I think of *Linton*? I had read *Earnshaw* twenty times for Linton). "I'm come home: I'd lost my way on the moor!" As it spoke, I discerned, obscurely, a child's face looking through the window. Terror made me cruel; and, finding it useless to attempt shaking the creature off, I pulled its wrist on to the broken pane, and rubbed it to and fro till the blood ran down and soaked the bedclothes: still it wailed, "Let me in!" and maintained its tenacious grip, almost maddening me with fear. "How can I!" I said at length. "Let *me* go, if you want me to let you in!" The fingers relaxed, I snatched mine through the hole, hurriedly piled the books up in a pyramid against it, and stopped my ears to exclude the lamentable prayer. I seemed to keep them closed above a quarter of an hour; yet, the instant I listened again, there was the doleful cry moaning on! "Begone!" I shouted, "I'll never let you in, not if you beg for twenty years." "It is twenty years," mourned the voice: "twenty years. I've been a waif for twenty years!" Thereat began a feeble scratching outside, and the pile of books moved as if thrust forward. I tried to jump up; but could not stir a limb; and so yelled aloud, in a frenzy of fright. To my confusion, I discovered the yell was not ideal: hasty footsteps approached my chamber door; somebody pushed it open, with a vigorous hand, and a light glimmered through the squares at the top of the bed. I sat shuddering yet, and wiping the perspiration from my forehead: the intruder appeared to hesitate, and muttered to himself. At last, he said in a half-whisper, plainly not expecting an answer, "Is anyone here?" I considered it best to confess my presence; for I knew Heathcliff's accents, and feared he might search further, if I kept quiet. With this intention, I turned and opened the panels. I shall not soon forget the effect my action produced.

Heathcliff stood near the entrance, in his shirt and trousers; with a candle dripping over his fingers, and his face as white as the wall behind him. The first creak of the oak startled him like an electric shock: the light leaped from his hold to a distance of some feet, and his agitation was so extreme, that he could hardly pick it up.

"It is only your guest, sir," I called out, desirous to spare him the humiliation of exposing his cowardice further. "I had the misfortune to scream in my sleep, owing to a frightful nightmare. I'm sorry I disturbed you."

"Oh, God confound you, Mr Lockwood! I wish you were at the —" commenced my host, setting the candle on a chair, because he found it impossible to hold it steady. "And who showed you up to this room?" he continued, crushing his nails into his palms, and grinding his teeth to subdue the maxillary convulsions. "Who was it? I've a good mind to turn them out of the house this moment!"

"It was your servant, Zillah," I replied, flinging myself on to the floor, and rapidly resuming my garments. "I should not care if you did, Mr Heathcliff; she richly deserves it. I suppose that she wanted to get another proof that the place was haunted, at my expense. Well, it is – swarming with ghosts and goblins! You have reason in shutting it up, I assure you. No one will thank you for a doze in such a den!"

"What do you mean?" asked Heathcliff, "and what are you doing? Lie down and finish out the night, since you *are* here; but, for Heaven's sake! don't repeat that horrid noise: nothing could excuse it, unless you were having your throat cut!"

"If the little fiend had got in at the window, she probably would have strangled me!" I returned. "I'm not going to endure the persecutions of your hospitable ancestors again. Was not the Reverend Jabes Branderham akin to you on the mother's side? And that minx, Catherine Linton, or Earnshaw, or however she was called – she must have been a changeling – wicked little soul! She told me she had been walking the earth these twenty years; a just punishment for her mortal transgressions, I've no doubt!"

Scarcely were these words uttered, when I recollected the association of Heathcliff's with Catherine's name in the book, which had completely slipped from my memory, till thus awakened. I blushed at my inconsideration; but without showing further consciousness of the offence, I hastened to add – "The truth is, sir, I passed the first part of the night in" – here I stopped afresh – I was about to say "perusing those old volumes", then it would have revealed my knowledge of their written, as well as their printed, contents; so, correcting myself, I went on – "in spelling over the name scratched on that window ledge. A monotonous occupation, calculated to set me asleep, like counting, or —"

"What *can* you mean by talking in this way to me?" thundered Heathcliff with savage vehemence. "How – how *dare* you, under my roof? – God! he's mad to speak so!" And he struck his forehead with rage.

I did not know whether to resent this language or pursue my explanation; but he seemed so powerfully affected that I took pity and proceeded with my dreams; affirming I had never heard the appellation of "Catherine Linton" before, but reading it often over produced an impression which personified itself when I had no longer my imagination under control. Heathcliff gradually fell back into the shelter of the bed, as I spoke; finally sitting down almost concealed behind it. I guessed, however, by his irregular and intercepted breathing, that he struggled to vanquish an excess of violent emotion. Not liking to show him that I heard the conflict, I continued my toilette rather noisily, looked at my watch, and soliloquized on the length of the night: "Not three o'clock yet! I could have taken oath it had been six. Time stagnates here: we must surely have retired to rest at eight!"

"Always at nine in winter, and always rise at four," said my host, suppressing a groan: and, as I fancied, by the motion of his shadow's arm, dashing a tear from his eyes. "Mr Lockwood," he added, "you may go into my room: you'll only be in the way, coming downstairs so early; and your childish outcry has sent sleep to the devil for me."

"And for me, too," I replied. "I'll walk in the yard till daylight, and then I'll be off; and you need not dread a repetition of my intrusion. I am now quite cured of seeking pleasure in society, be it country or town. A sensible man ought to find sufficient company in himself."

"Delightful company!" muttered Heathcliff. "Take the candle, and go where you please. I shall join you directly. Keep out of the yard, though, the dogs are unchained; and the house – Juno mounts sentinel there, and – nay, you can only ramble about the steps and passages. But, away with you! I'll come in two minutes!"

I obeyed, so far as to quit the chamber; when, ignorant where the narrow lobbies led, I stood still, and was witness, involuntarily, to a piece of superstition on the part of my landlord, which belied, oddly, his apparent sense. He got on to the bed, and wrenched open the lattice, bursting, as he pulled at it, into an uncontrollable passion of tears. "Come in! come in!" he sobbed. "Cathy, do come. Oh do – *once* more! Oh! my heart's darling! hear me *this* time, Catherine, at last!" The spectre showed a spectre's ordinary caprice; it gave no sign of being; but the snow and wind whirled wildly through, even reaching my station, and blowing out the light.

# THE GIRL WHO KISSED THE PEACH TREE

*An Italian folktale*

## ELEANOR FARJEON

AT LINGUAGLOSSA IN Sicily there once lived a little peasant girl called Marietta. It was a country full of fruit trees, peach, and apricot, and the bright persimmon; there were almond trees whose delicate pink flower came first of all in the year, and olive trees whose leaves were always green, and vineyards full of white and purple grapes in their season. The peasants' life depended on their fruit trees, the fruit trees were their fortune.

The fruit country lay spread out at the foot of a big mountain with a heart of fire, and a hole in the top. Sometimes the mountain was angry, and spat fire and red-hot stones into the air through the hole, and if it was *very* angry it went on for days, pouring out a fiery river of molten stone that flowed away over the top of the hole like porridge boiling over the pot; and flames leaped into the air, hundreds of feet high; and glowing lumps of rock were hurled through the flames, to fall where they would. All the while the fiery river streamed down the mountainside, destroying everything in its course, and making a desert of the pleasant land; and where it passed the air became so hot that no one could live or breathe in it. So the peasants who tilled the earth in the shadow of the mountain always lived in fear of the hour when the mountain should begin to mutter in its anger; and when it did, they prayed to Saint Anthony to appease the mountain's anger, and save their fruit trees from ruin.

The great anger did not come very often, and Marietta was seven years old before she heard the mountain mutter in one of its real tempers. There came a morning when Giacomo, her big brother, happened to be home for a day or so, and she was playing by herself on the plot of ground where her own little peach tree grew. This plot lay in the furthest corner of her brother's lands, and of all the fruit trees in those parts it grew closest to the mountain. Giacomo had planted it for her the day she was born, and she loved it better than anything else in the world. She would talk to it as if it were a friend, and Giacomo would sometimes tease her, and ask her how her playfellow was today.

"The little girl is feeling very happy," Marietta would answer, when the peach tree was in blossom; or perhaps, when the tree had peaches on it, she might say, "The little girl is very strong today." But later on, when the fruit was stripped and eaten, Marietta sometimes answered, "The little girl has gone away, she won't come out and play."

"What is she like, the little girl?" Giacomo would ask.

"So, *so* pretty; she laughs and sings, and dances all the time. She has a green dress and flowers on her head. She has gone to stay with the King of the Mountain, but she didn't want to go."

Then Giacomo would laugh a little, and pull Marietta's black curls, but old Lucia the grandmother, who lived in the house and cooked, would shake her head at him and mumble, "It may be so, it may be so, who knows?"

On this day when Giacomo was from home, while Marietta was picking flowers and chattering to her peach-tree she felt a sort of tremble in the earth, and heard a sort of grumble in the air. It was no more than she had heard and felt at other times, and all she said to herself was, *The King of the Mountain is angry about something.* But that sound brought men and women to a standstill at their work among the trees; and they gazed at the mountain with fear in their hearts.

After a while they knew that the thing they most feared was upon them. It might last a long while or a short while, but the fiery river had begun to pour over the mountaintop, and presently it would reach the fruitful plain.

That evening old Lucia said to Marietta, "Come."

"Where are we going?" asked Marietta.

"To the village, to pray to Saint Anthony. Bring flowers with you."

Marietta filled her little apron with the flowers she had gathered in the morning, and went with Lucia to the village. The peasants young and old were flocking there from all sides, and those who lived in the village had left their houses and were already in the church upon their knees. Nearly all had brought flowers, which they put at the feet of the figure of Saint Anthony.

Marietta, too, emptied her lapful before him, and then knelt down beside Lucia, and prayed.

"What shall I ask, Mamma Lucia?" she said.

"Ask that the fire may not descend upon us."

So Marietta prayed as she was bid, until she grew tired of kneeling; then she got up and found some of the village children playing in the black shadows behind the tall pillars in the church. She played with them, and presently fell asleep for a while, and then woke up again, and saw more peasants coming into the church, peasants from the mountainside, women in shawls, and men in old red cloaks lined with fur, bringing their children with them. Some had bundles of clothes and household goods, hastily got together before they fled from the fiery river which was descending on their homes.

All through the night the people stayed in the church, praying that the river might stop, or turn aside in its course, and in the early morning they went out and gazed towards the mountain. At the first glance they knew that their prayers had not availed, and that the fiery river was coming down on their lands. Already the air was scorching hot with its approach.

Old Lucia threw up her hands and wailed, and so did many others. Then the priest said, "Have faith, my children!" and bade some of the men bring out the statue of Saint Anthony, and place it in the open air in the path of the fiery river. The men went into the church, and came out carrying the statue; and they bore it through the village, and set it on the road where the priest directed. The women and children followed with the flowers, and they heaped the flowers about the figure of the Saint, and gathered more to cover his feet.

Then in the clear dawn, with the hot breath of the mountain rolling towards them, the people all knelt down in the road, and the priest lifted his hands and prayed again to heaven to turn the course of the fire aside.

And still the fire streamed on.

At last the priest turned to the people and said with tears in his eyes, "My children, a miracle may still happen, but I cannot let you stay here any longer. The danger is too great. You must leave your homes and your trees to heaven's mercy, and go."

The peasants rose up full of sorrow. They went to their houses and got a few things to carry with them, and before they left, they went out into their orchards and kissed their fruit trees. Then in a great crowd they went out on the roads, and hurried away from the homes they never expected to see again. On every road was a stream of men flying from the stream of fire. Lucia and Marietta went with the rest.

Presently Lucia felt her dress tugged. "Mamma Lucia! Mamma Lucia!" said Marietta.

The grandmother looked down. "What is it, my little one?"

"Mamma Lucia, why did they kiss the trees?"

"To bless them, and save them, if it is God's will."

"Mamma Lucia, I did not kiss my peach tree."

"The poor little peach tree!" sighed old Lucia. "It will be the first to go."

"I must go back and kiss it, Mamma Lucia."

"No, no, that is impossible now. It cannot be helped. Only

feel, the air grows hotter. We must go as fast as we can."

And old Lucia went as fast as she could, in the crowd that pressed about her – and in the press one little body at her side was like another little body, and she felt a child clinging to her skirts and thought no more about it. She only thought of the need to hurry on, until she heard her own name being called out loud along the road. "Mamma Lucia! Mamma Lucia! Where are you? Are you there? Where is Mamma Lucia?"

"Here I am, here I am," said the old woman, and "Here she is!" cried a dozen voices, and many hands pushed her forward, till she was face to face with Giacomo, who on his way home had seen the great crowd coming towards him, and the fiery stream upon the mountain which would eat up his house and lands. But he was not thinking at that moment of his house, he was thinking of his little sister Marietta. When he saw Lucia his brow cleared, and he said, "Heaven be praised! Where is the child?"

"Here she is," said the old woman, and pulled forward the little one who clutched her skirts – and it was not Marietta; it was Stefano, the hunchback's child.

"Why, what is this?" exclaimed Lucia in bewilderment. "Where is Marietta?" And she called Marietta's name, and the crowd called too, but in vain, Marietta was not there.

Suddenly Lucia threw up her hands and cried, "I know! I know! The Saints have mercy! She has gone back to kiss her peach tree." The grandmother turned hurriedly and stumbled through the crowd, that made a way for her and Giacomo, whose heart was beating heavily with fear. Scarcely noticing the heat like a furnace into which they were hastening, the big man and the old woman went with all their speed along the road to the mountain. They passed the village, they passed the figure of Saint Anthony among his flowers, they passed many orchards and vineyards belonging to their neighbours, and at last they came to their own place at the mountain-foot. They did not stay to look inside the house; in spite of the heat they went across the lands to the far corner where Marietta's peach tree grew.

And there lying under it they found her, her arm around it, her cheek pressed against it, her eyes fast closed. Beside her was a tiny image of Saint Anthony, which always stood in Mamma Lucia's room, and which Marietta had set in front of the tree, with a handful of flowers at his feet.

Giacomo stooped down over his little sister, and said, "She is asleep. Her skin is cool."

"Heaven be praised!" said Mamma Lucia. "And the air is no hotter, too."

They looked once more towards the mountain, and saw to their amazement that at the foot the fiery flood had turned aside, and after creeping a little way along the border of their lands, had ceased to flow.

"It is the miracle," said old Lucia.

Marietta stirred, opened her eyes, and saw her big brother bending over her. She jumped up and flung her arms around his neck.

"Giacomo! Oh, how glad I am to see you! Giacomo, what do you think happened while you were away? The King of the

Mountains got angry and sent down a river of fire, and I went to the church and gave flowers to Saint Anthony, and I was in the church all night, Giacomo, with the others! And in the morning we went out and put Saint Anthony on the road, and knelt down till it was too hot, and then everybody kissed the trees and ran away, but I forgot to kiss my peach tree, Giacomo, so I came back and brought Saint Anthony to protect her, and then I kissed her and it was so hot I was frightened, but the little girl said, 'Don't be afraid, Marietta, the King of the Mountains will go back if only I go back with him, and I *will* go back because *you* came back to kiss me, so go to sleep, go to sleep, Marietta, don't be afraid.' So I did go to sleep, and where is the King of the Mountain?"

Giacomo said, "He has gone back, Marietta," and he hugged her close and looked at Lucia over her head. And the old woman looked at him and at Marietta, and at the peach tree and the mountain, and she mumbled, "It may be so, it may be so, who knows?"

# THE THING IN THE POND
## PAUL ERNST

IT WAS LATE afternoon when Gordon Sharpe, tall, lean, and bearded, got out of the hired car at the door of Professor Weidbold's country house. He lifted out his grips and his gun case.

"That must be a right sizeable shootin' iron, mister," the driver drawled.

"It's stopped quite a few elephants in its time," replied Sharpe, with his steel-blue eyes twinkling.

The driver glanced oddly at him. "Well, there ain't any elephants around here, but this is a funny part of Florida, mister, just the same."

Sharpe's thick black beard stirred with a grin. "I read about it in the papers last night," he said. "Got a monster or something, down this way, haven't you?"

"That's what they say. Me – I don't take no stock in it."

The hired car rattled off. The door opened, and Weidbold's servant came out of the house. Sharpe stared at him. He was small, quiet, efficient. Quite different from old Sam Klegg, the sulky, not-too-clean loafer Weidbold had had working for him when Sharpe last visited here.

The man reached for the grips and the gun case.

"I'll carry that," said Sharpe. "Where's the professor?"

"He's out by the pond," replied the servant. "I'll show you to your room and then tell him you're here."

Sharpe went upstairs with the man. When he was alone, he stepped to the window.

His room was at the rear of the combined house and laboratory. Twenty acres of weeds and neglect stretched before his eyes from the house to a small, marshy puddle called Greer's Pond. Sharpe remembered this as a stagnant pool, fed by seepage, heated to blood warmth by the Florida sun. It was rather deep, and it teemed with small life.

He could see the sluggish glint of the water now, and, at one end, the stoop-shouldered, shambling figure of Professor Weidbold. Then he saw the servant start across the fields and noted his trim, precise walk. The man contrasted humorously with the surly ruffian, Sam Klegg, who had worked here ten years ago.

Sharpe went downstairs to the laboratory. Weidbold spent most of his waking hours here. He would expect to meet his ex-pupil there.

The tanned, powerful African explorer blinked as he entered the cool dimness of the laboratory. Then he saw that all was unchanged.

There was the delicate device for registering the minute quantities of electricity generated by a growing plant. There was the little glass case in which Weidbold had kept a bit of muscle from the heart of a chicken, a lump no larger than the head of a match, living and growing in a salt solution for sixteen years. Here was the complicated apparatus with which Weidbold increased the chlorophyll content in plants with ultra-violet rays. Then came cases of zoological monstrosities – newts with three eyes, salamanders with tails where their legs should be, and heads grafted on where their tails should be.

The door of the laboratory opened.

"Gordon!" exclaimed Professor Weidbold, coming in. "It's good to see you again. You're looking fine."

"Nothing seems changed," said Sharpe heartily. "I might have stepped out yesterday instead of ten years ago. The only new thing is your servant. You fired Sam Klegg at last, eh?"

"Yes," said the professor, a muscle twitching in his cheek. "A few weeks after you'd left. I wrote you about it, I think."

"You did. And you wrote me, too, that the sullen fellow took a mean revenge by dumping several casks of chemicals and some of your most valuable laboratory equipment into Greer's Pond."

The professor looked so distressed that Sharpe put his big arm affectionately over the thin shoulders.

"It's ancient history now," he said. Then, "Why on earth did you ask me to bring an elephant gun when I came for the visit? Are you going into ballistics now?"

Weidbold did not smile back. "Not exactly," he murmured, avoiding Sharpe's gaze.

"Then," Sharpe returned, laughing, "it must be you wanted me to use it on the monster in your pool."

Professor Weidbold did not smile at this, either. "So you've heard," he said.

"I've heard of little else in the last twenty-four hours," Sharpe responded, gazing at the professor with worried eyes. "The Associated Press got the story. The whole country is laughing at the hoax. You'll probably have pilgrims to Greer's Pond by the thousands in a few days."

"What did the papers say about the – the hoax?"

Sharpe lighted his pipe, his eyes continuing to probe Weidbold's. "The New York papers say there is a dinosaur alive down here. The Chicago sheets think it's a sea serpent. But of course nobody really believes there's anything cooped up in your spoonful of water. It's just another tall tale, like that of the monster in the Scottish loch some time."

Again the muscle twitched in Weidbold's cheek. Sharpe's fingers tightened on the bowl of his pipe. The old man looked as if he actually put credence in this silly story of a monster in Greer's Pond. He must have broken recently in mind as well as in health not to laugh with a scientist's scepticism at such talk.

A monster! In Greer's Pond!

"Of course there may actually be some big beast, like an alligator, in the pool," said Sharpe, keeping his tone light. "It'll be sport to find out. We'll go hunting tomorrow. We'll take your spaniel, Spot –"

"Spot's dead," Weidbold interrupted heavily.

Sharpe whistled. "Too bad! Run over by an automobile?"

"No," said Weidbold; "drowned. In Greer's Pond. It was three nights ago. I heard him barking as if his throat would split out by the pond. Then, suddenly, the barking ceased."

The professor stared abstractedly at a glass case in which a curious monstrosity, a newt with two heads, from an egg cell half divided in embryo, was preserved.

"I went back to sleep, thinking little of it. But the next morning Spot didn't appear, so I wandered over to the pond. I saw his tracks in the soft mud next to the water's edge. They went into the water and disappeared."

"That sounds like a 'gator, all right," Sharpe nodded. "They go for dogs."

"An alligator?" mused Weidbold. "Possibly. But Raeburn, who owns the land behind mine, doesn't think so. He thinks that if a big alligator was in the pool, it would be seen often on the surface of the water or on the bank. And Raeburn has never actually seen anything. Nor have I."

"Why not drain the pond?" asked Sharpe.

Weidbold sighed. "I am a poor man. Due to the lie of the land, draining would cost more than my entire fortune." He cleared his throat. "Come on out and look around now, will you? I saw something rather interesting this noon. I was out looking at it again when you arrived."

"Certainly," said Sharpe. "Shall I take my gun?"

He had tried to make his voice careless, but some tone in it must have sounded wrong.

"You think I'm a little mad, don't you?" said Weidbold. "Well, no matter. Come along."

They went out by the laboratory door and started across the neglected acreage behind the house to Greer's Pond. Far off was the country road. They saw several cars slow down as they passed.

"Sightseers will be swarming here pretty soon to look at the monster in the pond," predicted Sharpe.

Weidbold shivered as if he were cold. "I know. Dozens of people crowding around the edge of the pool – something must be done at once."

They reached the scum-flecked pond. Sharpe remembered it well. He and Weidbold had seined out many a wriggling subject for laboratory experimentation. Oddly, he saw no small life now.

"Here," said Weidbold, in a low, strained tone. "This is what I wanted to show you."

Sharpe gazed where the old professor pointed. He saw cow tracks – ordinary cow tracks etched in the mud by the water. A fresh wave of pity for Weidbold grew in his breast.

Then he moistened his lips as he peered closer at the tracks, and he forgot to pity Weidbold so tolerantly.

The cow tracks led from the property on Raeburn's side of the pond to the edge of the pool. Indistinct till they reached the mud, they were only too clear there.

The tracks were deep. They were slurred and close-bunched. The animal that had made them had been pulling back frantically, straining back with deep-planted hoofs from the water and being inexorably hauled into it just the same.

"It must have been a monster 'gator," muttered Sharpe stubbornly. "It *must* have been –"

But there were no 'gator tracks anywhere to be seen.

Instead, half-effacing the cow tracks in some places, there was something the like of which he had never observed in all his big-game hunting days.

The mud around some of the cow tracks had been pressed flat and smooth as if a heavy, fat body had slithered across there.

"Here comes my neighbour," he heard Weidbold say.

He looked up and saw a man approaching them. He was a big, burly fellow in faded blue overalls. He was striding towards them aggressively, swiftly, glaring at the professor as he came.

"I might have knowed I should look here first for my cow," he shouted when he was still fifty yards from them. "Spent the hull day phoning around to see if she'd gone into someone else's barn. But I should have knowed where she'd disappeared to!"

He reached them with the last words and took just one look at the tracks. His black eyes glittered with rage.

"Perfessor," he grated, "what the hell's *in* this pond? What in tarnation" – he glared at the tracks – "can drag a full-grown Guernsey down into the water?"

"Who knows, Raeburn!" said Weidbold, his old voice trembling. "I lost my dog, you know, a few nights ago."

"It's probably a 'gator," Sharpe offered.

Raeburn whirled on him. "A 'gator! Whoever you are and wherever you come from, I reckon you must know better than that. You don't see any tracks, do you? And nobody's ever seen one sunnin' itself, have they? And what would one 'gator do with a hull cow?"

He whirled back to Weidbold, and his voice tensed Sharpe's muscles angrily.

"Perfessor, we've been mighty tolerant around here about the devil's work you do alone in that laboratory of your'n. We ain't said nothing and we ain't done nothing, though we all knew your work was agin' nature. Now I reckon it's time to think of acting. You know – there has been folks lynched around this part of the country."

Sharpe's fists clenched, but he remembered that this man had just lost a valuable animal.

"Why do you talk like that to me?" faltered the old professor. "Whatever is in this pond —"

"Perfessor," Raeburn interrupted, "you know what's in that pond! I don't, and no one else does – but you do. I can see it in your face. I been seein' it there for a month."

"I assure you —" mumbled Weidbold.

But Raeburn didn't stop to hear. He turned on his heel and walked away.

Sharpe gazed at Weidbold.

"You see," murmured the professor wearily, "I have something actual to fear, regardless of what may or may not be in that slimy water."

Sharpe's gaze held steady. "What *is* in there, Professor?"

"I – I haven't the faintest idea. As a scientist I simply cannot admit that —"

"What?" Sharpe rapped out, as the old man stopped.

"Nothing." Weidbold sighed. And he would say no more.

Sharpe turned from him to stare at the pond again.

Covered in spots with green scum, clear in spots like a black mirror, the surface of the opaque water lay without a ripple to feather it. The eye could not penetrate more than a foot or so down into the motionless, silt-filled pool.

Sharpe stared harder.

No movement? No ripples? But there were.

In the centre of the pond a faint stir of water grew regularly into being – so faint that Sharpe had not caught it till now. It ringed out, wider and wider, barely stirring the scum, till it reached the shores.

In slow, rhythmic succession, the ripples ringed from the centre of the pond to stir at last along the shore. As if something down under there was breathing, with a slow heave of sides or gills. Or as if a mighty heart was beating down there, with each slow pulsation registering on the recording surface of the pool. That was more apt. The water was stirring regularly, like a huge, slow pulse.

Sharpe's fingernails pressed into the palms of his hands; but his voice was even as he said, "Got any meat in your refrigerator?"

Weidbold glanced at him quickly. It was impossible to guess whether his old eyes had been alert enough to catch the steady stir of the water.

"I have a slab of bacon and some beef," he said.

"Good!" Sharpe's voice was incisive. "We won't wait till tomorrow to hunt. Visitors might be crowding in by then, and that might be – unhealthy. Would you mind stepping to the house and asking your man to bring my gun and the meat here to me?"

Weidbold nodded and turned away. Sharpe watched him shamble across the field, then turned back to watch the enigmatic surface of the pond. Down in its mysterious, black depths —

Weidbold brought the meat and gun back himself. Sharpe frowned at him.

"No need for you to stay around, sir. Nothing may rise to this bait at all, since the cow was dragged in so recently."

"I will stay," said the old professor.

"There might be danger —"

"I will stay, Gordon."

Sharpe shrugged, and loaded the big gun. They went to the edge of the pond, not speaking to each other, not looking at each other.

Sharpe threw the slab of bacon as near to the centre of the pool as he could. It splashed in the green scum.

There was no answering splash. Ripples welled out from the disturbance and gradually subsided. That was all.

"It – it might be that the – the thing has such a low nervous organization that it can't tell when food or prey is near," faltered Weidbold. His face was white and his hands were shaking.

"We might ask the cow what her opinion is," said Sharpe.

He picked up the chunk of beef and sent it after the bacon. It hit the scum even nearer the centre of the pool.

The slimy surface of the pond boiled a little near the meat. It seemed to hump up slightly. Grimly, silently, the commotion in the water grew. With strained intensity the two men stared.

Something broke the surface of the pond; something that was pallidly pink and smooth and glistening; something that was hollowed in the centre like a gigantic cup.

The monstrous cup closed around the meat just as Sharpe's gun roared out. Both men saw a hole torn in the pink fringe of the cup. Both men saw the fringe continue to clamp down over the meat as if nothing had happened. Then the thing sank silently under the water. There was a soft sucking noise as an eddy whirled above. The eddy died down and there was nothing.

Sharpe wiped the palms of his hands on his trouser legs.

"It didn't even feel it!" he breathed, his eyes wide and staring. "A slug that would have stopped an elephant, and it didn't even feel it!"

Weidbold's trembling fingers were plucking at his lips.

"Like firing into a sofa cushion," Sharpe went on. "No chance for the explosive bullet to get in its work. It simply tore through —"

He stopped abruptly. Weidbold's hand clutched convulsively at his arm. The two glared at the water before them.

A commotion was growing there. Once again the green scum was humping upwards as something sluggishly sought the surface. And the commotion rippled the stagnant, warm water in a straight line for the spot where Sharpe and Weidbold stood.

With a hoarse exclamation, Sharpe jerked his arm from the professor's clutch and ripped the bolt of his gun out and back.

He levelled it towards the seething water.

The surface of the water broke at last, almost at their feet. Something pallidly pink shone wet and sleek above the green scum. It was coming steadily through the water towards them.

It reached the shore – rather, the front of it reached the shore. The rear of it trailed back out of sight in the black water. It began, with a queer hitching movement, to climb out onto the mud.

Something roughly oblong and flat, like an undulating pink blanket – something that was simply a blind, sluggish lump, without limbs or tentacles, exuding mucus to protect its tender-looking surface from twigs and pebbles in the mud.

As the thing crawled farther and farther up on the bank it seemed to slough off chunks of itself. But in an instant it was apparent that the chunks were half-dissolved bits of meat. A horn dropped, and some whitened bones, and the skull of a cow.

"Shoot!" cried the professor.

Sharpe only stood there, peering over his sights at the thing. It hitched towards them, progressing by humping itself up in folds and then straightening out – expanding and contracting in rhythmic waves of movement. And still its bulk trailed endlessly from the pond.

"*Shoot!*" screeched Weidbold.

Sharpe pressed the trigger.

Again the heavy-calibre gun roared out in the silent afternoon. Again a big bullet tore into the viscous, tender-looking pink mass. And again it sliced right through, with not enough resistance offered for the explosion of the bullet.

A jagged hole, oozing straw-coloured fluid, yawned in the loathsome pinkish mass. The bulk of it stirred as the bullet exploded in the mud beneath. But it kept on coming.

Both men ran, sweat streaming down their faces – ran as if pursued by fiends.

A hundred yards away they stopped and looked back.

There was a subsiding commotion at the water's edge. Something flipped sluggishly up from the green scum and then sank.

"Maybe – it's dead," quavered Professor Weidbold.

Sharpe drew a long breath, and then began to stride purposefully towards the house.

"You know better than that," he said quietly. "That thing could never die. It could be blown to bits and still not die. Because it isn't alive; not as a complete organism, anyhow. It has no nervous system; it has no vital organs; it simply has cellular, multifarious life. Isn't that right, Professor?"

Weidbold said nothing. He hurried to keep pace with Sharpe's long strides.

"What are you going to do, Gordon?" he asked as they neared the house.

"I'm going to do some telephoning," he said. "I am going to order some dynamite and about a carload of sulphuric acid, and I'm going to have a contractor come out first thing in the morning. We'll dynamite the pool at dawn. Then the contractor can put up a high fence. After that we'll sluice the pool with sulphuric acid and keep sluicing it. That's the only way I can think of to destroy utterly the thing in the pond. And if it isn't destroyed," he added grimly, "I see no reason why it shouldn't keep on growing indefinitely, till it's the size of a ten-storey building. Do you?"

Weidbold only looked at him, miserably, imploringly.

Next morning, with pearl first streaking the east, the two went back to the pond. Sharpe walked carefully, carrying half a dozen sticks of dynamite tied in a bundle with a short fuse attached.

The pond looked like a great, green-flecked fire opal in the early morning. Sharpe stared at it. Off-centre a little, perhaps thirty yards from where they stood, a faint ripple formed regularly on the still surface, to ring the stagnant water and subside gently on the shores. Beat, beat, beat.

Sharpe lit the fuse and threw the bundle of dynamite.

It fell with a splash in the centre of the rhythmic ripples. Both men ran from the pool, covering their ears, holding their mouths open.

There was a thunderous roar before they had taken twenty steps. They were knocked from their feet.

Water and mud rained down on them. Water and mud, and something else – fragments of pallid, pinkish substance that struck down on them like clammy hands, to plop off onto the ground, and to begin at once, with queer, humping movements, to slide back to the boiling, half-empty pond.

Alive, but not alive! Frightful, blind growth, as vital and indestructible as the living, primal ooze!

"No death for it but utter annihilation," muttered Sharpe.

"But it will be weeks before any of the pieces can become dangerously big. Long before that we'll have the place burned out with acid."

The two got up slowly. Sharpe looked at the professor for a long time.

"I know what you're thinking," said Weidbold. "But it can't be true. It can't! By all the laws of biology it can't —"

"Professor," said Sharpe, "it was about ten years ago that your discharged servant got back at you by dumping that laboratory stuff into the pool, wasn't it?"

"Yes," said the old man, his lips twitching.

"Among the stuff was a lot of sodium, potassium, and calcium salts, and probably a barrel of sugar," guessed Sharpe.

"Y-yes," admitted Weidbold.

"Now, while I was here ten years ago you cut off a bit of that chicken-heart muscle you've kept living and pulsing for sixteen years in a solution of potassium, calcium, sodium, and sugar. I remember that distinctly. You've cut off several bits; otherwise the stuff would outgrow the nourishment-capacity of the case. What happened to that fragment?"

"I – it got lost, or something."

"It's conceivable that it was among the stuff your servant dumped into the pond, isn't it?"

"Such a fantastic accident —" mumbled Weidbold.

"All accidents are fantastic," said Sharpe curtly. "That's why they call them accidents. It's conceivable – isn't it?"

Weidbold nodded.

"And in this warm, life-filled pond," Sharpe pursued

relentlessly, "the tiny bit of muscle substance flourished. It absorbed the chemicals freakishly dumped in with it, and finally all the small life. Then it began to reach out for more food in its voracious growth."

"I tell you it's almost impossible!" shrieked the professor. "It could not live outside a laboratory! Ask any scientist —"

"I'd prefer to ask Raeburn's cow or your dog," Sharpe cut in dryly.

Weidbold spread his hands in a defeated gesture. "Gordon," he said in a different tone, "I am an old man. I have neither the money nor the energy to move to another part of the country and set up my laboratory all over again – which I'd have to do if the people around here believed that some experiment in my laboratory really was responsible for – this. Now – you see how impossible it is that a tiny bit of flesh from the heart of a dead chicken could grow to a thing like – like that, don't you?"

Sharpe watched the last of the small pink fragments fold over on itself on its way to the water of Greer's Pond. The little fragment slipped sluggishly under the green scum of the surface.

"We'll say it's impossible," he conceded at last.

# SMART ICE CREAM
## PAUL JENNINGS

WELL, I CAME top of the class again. One hundred out of one hundred for maths. And one hundred out of one hundred for English. I'm just a natural brain, the best there is. There isn't one kid in the class who can come near me. Next to me they are all dumb.

Even when I was a baby I was smart. The day that I was born my mother started tickling me. "Bub, bub, bub," she said.

"Cut it out, Mum," I told her. "That tickles." She nearly fell out of bed when I said that. I was very advanced for my age.

Every year I win a lot of prizes: top of the class, top of the school, stuff like that. I won a prize for spelling when I was only three years old. I am a terrific speller. If you can say it, I can spell it. Nobody can trick me on spelling. I can spell every word there is.

Some kids don't like me; I know that for a fact. They say I'm a show-off. I don't care. They are just jealous because they are not as clever as me. I'm good looking too. That's another reason why they are jealous.

Last week something bad happened. Another kid got one hundred out of one hundred for maths too. That never happened before – no one has ever done as well as me. I am always first on my own. A kid called Jerome Dadian beat me. He must have cheated. I was sure he cheated. It had something to do with that ice cream. I was sure of it. I decided to find out what was going on; I wasn't going to let anyone pull a fast one on me.

It all started with the ice cream man. Mr Peppi. The old fool had a van which he parked outside the school. He sold ice cream, all different types. He had every flavour there is, and some that I had never heard of before.

He didn't like me very much. He told me off once. "Go to the back of the queue," he said. "You pushed in."

"Mind your own business, Pop," I told him. "Just hand over the ice cream."

"No," he said. "I won't serve you unless you go to the back."

I went round to the back of the van, but I didn't get in the queue. I took out a nail and made a long scratch on his rotten old van. He had just had it painted. Peppi came and had a look. Tears came into his eyes. "You are a bad boy," he said. "One day you will get into trouble. You think you are smart. One day you will be too smart."

I just laughed and walked off. I knew he wouldn't do anything. He was too soft-hearted. He was always giving free ice creams to kids that had no money. He felt sorry for poor people. The silly fool.

There were a lot of stories going round about that ice cream. People said that it was good for you. Some kids said that it made you better when you were sick. One of the teachers called it "Happy Ice Cream". I didn't believe it; it never made me happy.

All the same, there was something strange about it. Take Pimples Peterson for example. That wasn't his real name – I just called him that because he had a lot of pimples. Anyway, Peppi heard me calling Peterson "Pimples". "You are a real mean boy," he said. "You are always picking on some one else, just because they are not like you."

"Get lost, Peppi," I said. "Go and flog your ice cream somewhere else."

Peppi didn't answer me. Instead he spoke to Pimples. "Here, eat this," he told him. He handed Peterson an ice cream. It was the biggest ice cream I had ever seen. It was coloured purple. Peterson wasn't too sure about it. He didn't think he had enough money for such a big ice cream.

"Go on," said Mr Peppi. "Eat it. I am giving it to you for nothing. It will get rid of your pimples."

I laughed and laughed. Ice cream doesn't get rid of pimples, it *gives* you pimples. Anyway, the next day when Peterson came to school he had no pimples. Not one. I couldn't believe it. The ice cream had cured his pimples.

There were some other strange things that happened too. There was a kid at the school who had a long nose. Boy, was it long. He looked like Pinocchio. When he blew it you could hear it a mile away. I called him "Snozzle". He didn't like being called Snozzle. He used to go red in the face when I said it, and that was every time that I saw him. He didn't say anything back – he was scared that I would punch him up.

Peppi felt sorry for Snozzle too. He gave him a small green ice cream every morning, for nothing. What a jerk. He never gave me a free ice cream.

You won't believe what happened but I swear it's true. Snozzle's nose began to grow smaller. Every day it grew a bit smaller. In the end it was just a normal nose. When it was the right size Peppi stopped giving him the green ice creams.

I made up my mind to put a stop to this ice cream business. Jerome Dadian had been eating ice cream the day he got one hundred for maths. It must have been the ice cream making him smart. I wasn't going to have anyone doing as well as me. I was the smartest kid in the school, and that's the way I wanted it to stay. I wanted to get a look inside that ice cream van to find out what was going on.

I knew where Peppi kept his van at night – he left it in a small lane behind his house. I waited until about eleven o'clock at night. Then I crept out of the house and down to Peppi's van. I took a crowbar, a bucket of sand, a torch and some bolt cutters with me.

There was no one around when I reached the van. I sprang the door open with the crowbar and shone my torch around inside. I had never seen so many tubs of ice cream before. There was every flavour you could think of: there was apple and banana, cherry and mango, blackberry and watermelon and about fifty other flavours. Right at the end of the van were four bins with locks on them. I went over and had a look. It was just as I thought – these were his special flavours. Each one had writing on the top. This is what they said:

HAPPY ICE CREAM for cheering people up.
NOSE ICE CREAM for long noses.
PIMPLE ICE CREAM for removing pimples.
SMART ICE CREAM for smart alecs.

Now I knew his secret. That rat Dadian had been eating Smart Ice Cream; that's how he got one hundred for maths. I knew there couldn't be anyone as clever as me. I decided to fix Peppi up once and for all. I took out the bolt cutters and cut the locks off the four bins; then I put sand into every bin in the van. Except for the Smart Ice Cream. I didn't put any sand in that.

I laughed to myself. Peppi wouldn't sell much ice cream now. Not unless he started a new flavour – Sand Ice Cream. I looked at the Smart Ice Cream. I decided to eat some; it couldn't do any harm. Not that I needed it – I was already about as smart as you could get. Anyway, I gave it a try. I ate the lot. Once I started I couldn't stop. It tasted good. It was delicious.

I left the van and went home to bed, but I couldn't sleep. To tell the truth, I didn't feel too good. So I decided to write this. Then if any funny business has been going on, you people will know what happened. I think I have made a mistake. I don't think Dadian did get any Smart Ice Cream.

It iz the nekst day now. Somefing iz hapening to me. I don't feal quite az smart. I have bean trying to do a reel hard sum. It iz wun and wun. Wot duz wun and wun make? Iz it free or iz it for?

# THE PELICAN

## ANN PILLING

THE CASTLE STOOD on a great rock with a twisty flight of steps going up to it from the car park, a hundred and ninety-nine steps the guide book said, and the children intended to count them all. They could see very little that day. The village, and the castle high above it, shimmered through sheets of rain, and the low clouds were caught on the towers like rags, making it look like the palace of the wicked queen in some old fairy tale.

Tom and Gillian stood in the rain and looked round. The only vehicle in the car park, apart from theirs, was a van with one wheel missing. Even the ticket collector had gone home.

"I hate this," Tom said. "Why did we have to come? Why couldn't we stay in the flat? At least we could have watched *Tiswas.*"

"We didn't come all the way to Northumberland just to watch television," Dad said rather irritably. "There's plenty to see here, when the rain eases off."

"I wanted to go swimming," Tom grumbled.

"I wish you'd shut up," Gillian said. "You've been in the water nearly every day. Anyway, nobody swims in weather like this. You are ridiculous."

"I'm not."

"You are."

"Those steps look awfully slippery," Mum said. "The water's just pouring down them, look. I don't fancy climbing up there, not in this."

"Let's go into the church then," Dad suggested. "It'll stop soon."

At the word "church" seven-year-old Tom went rigid. Rainy days on holiday meant being dragged round museums and stately homes, where all he could see was the bottom of somebody's anorak. And churches! He disliked them most of all. They were always chilly, and smelt nasty.

Everyone was feeling wet and cold, not just Tom. Gillian knew that her father was about to lose his temper. "Come on," she said grabbing Tom's hand and running across the car park with him. "At least it'll be dry inside."

In the church someone was playing the organ. The two children wandered aimlessly up and down the pews while their parents read the notices on the pictures and old carvings, and looked at the memorials. Then Tom spotted something at the front, and ran up to a brass lectern that held an enormous Bible.

He said, "Isn't it funny?"

It looked as though whoever had made it had changed his mind halfway through the design. The outstretched wings were those an eagle but the head was grotesque, wrenched awkwardly sideways to show a feathered profile. This bird was all beak, and there was a great bag underneath, dropping down from a head that looked too puny to support it. It was a pelican.

Tom was laughing at it, then Gillian said, "Look, there's a bird over there too."

In the middle of the west window there was a pelican in stained glass. The bird stood on a nest full of open beaks and it was strangely twisted over, with its beak buried deep in its breast. Bright drops of blood sprayed down onto the heads of the fledglings and something was written underneath, in ancient letters:

*And so hir pelican*
*Of hir lyfe blud*
*Yaf to hir chickes*
*And help them with its gud.*

"What on earth does that mean?"

"The pelican gives its blood to feed its young," Dad said, looking at his guide book. "It says it's an old Christian symbol, but that it's really nothing to do with pelicans; it says it should be a flamingo, or something. It's a quaint idea anyway."

"Ugh," Tom said. "I think it's horrible."

A young man came down from the organ and went out, leaving the door open, and the children followed him. It was fresh-smelling outside.

"It's not raining so heavily now, Dad," Gillian said. "Can we climb up to the castle?"

"All right, but we'll have to go carefully, and I don't

suppose we'll see much from the top. I think we can go round the side of the church, and join the steps a bit higher up."

They all walked through the churchyard, slipping in the mud. The path ended quite suddenly at a stone wall with a gate in it, and they were looking down a wooded river valley through which the water slid greyly, parting the green dimness of the trees like hair.

"It must be a marvellous view when it's clear," Mum was saying, but Gillian interrupted. "Look, down there, on the bank. That pink thing. It's a statue." Dad got out his binoculars and focussed.

"Well I'm blowed," he said. "Look through these, Gill."

Through the misty rings she could see the figure of a bird. There was no mistaking the long scrawny neck and the bulging beak. It was another pelican. Tom grabbed at the glasses.

"Don't do that, Tom, you'll break them."

"Ouch! Don't pinch my arm!"

The cry echoed down the still valley, and the bird on the flat stone moved suddenly; it opened ragged wings then took off, flapping clumsily downstream.

"Look at that," Mum said. "I can't believe it."

"What do you think it was?" Gillian whispered. "It really did look just like —"

Then a voice behind them said, "I know what you're talking about. You must have seen the pelican." It was the young man they had seen in the church.

"We did see something down there. I thought it might be

a statue, then it flew off. Could it have been a heron?"

"No, it's a pelican."

Mum said, "But where did it come from?" and Tom shouted out, "You don't get pelicans in England, except in zoos."

"That's right. We don't know. It just appeared on the river bank, a year or so ago, and settled down here. They think it must have been migrating and that it got blown off course somehow. It's quite happy here. It flies up and down the river and keeps an eye on things. He's quite a character, Percy is."

"Percy?"

"That's right. The castle up there once belonged to the great Percy family, so it seemed just the right name for him. Have you been up there yet?"

"We were on our way, but it's so wet."

"I'd wait for a drier day if I were you, then you can see everything. You can row down from here to the hermitage, it's a stone cell cut out of the rock, and there's a good walk by the river, along that path; The Butts, it's called."

"Can you swim there?" Tom asked.

"You can, so long as you know what you're doing. Are you a good swimmer, then?"

"I've just done my hundred metres."

In the quietness the pelican had returned to its stone. Gillian watched as it folded its wings in after landing, and started pecking at its breast, like the one in the church window.

She said, "How strange that Percy should come here – I

mean, to this church, with the lectern and everything."

"It is strange. Everyone's interested in Percy. The vicar can tell you more, he's quite fond of him. I don't suppose we'll ever know where he came from, or why."

The day they returned, nobody could see the pelican. Gillian wanted to wait around for him, on the bank, but Tom was impatient. It was a glorious day and Dad had promised him a swim in the open-air pool that afternoon, when they got back to the holiday flat. They were going to practise straddle jumps.

There was only one boat, and it was out for the day, so they walked along The Butts and ate their picnic at the hermitage, a curious deep cell cut out of a massive sandstone bank. There was nobody else there. Tom and Gillian ran in and out, shouting loudly to make echoes, and standing under the drips that ran off the dank walls.

"Stay just like that!" Dad shouted. "In the doorway. It's a really good shot." Then, "Oh damn!"

"What's the matter?"

"I've left my camera up at the church. I must have. I took a couple of pictures from that wall, of the view down the valley. We'll have to go straight back, I'm sorry. Come on."

"It'll still be there," Mum said. "It won't take us long."

They packed the picnic away hurriedly and got up, but Dad was worrying. It was a new, very expensive camera.

"Look, we'll walk on ahead, the children will be all right. We'll meet you in the car park. Don't be too long though. Keep your eye on Tom, Gillian."

"OK," Gillian said flatly, not wanting to be left on her own with Tom. He could be a little devil sometimes.

And sure enough, the minute his parents were properly out of sight he got his wicked look, and began to scramble down the slithery path to the water's edge.

"I'm going to swim," he announced. He started to walk along the bank, peeling his clothes off as he went, until he was in his swimming trunks, looking down into a wide, shallow pool. He dipped a toe in. "It's not bad. The sun's been on it."

"Tom. You can't. You should never swim in rivers, and Dad'll be furious. He's taking you to the pool anyway, when we get back."

"Oh shut up. It's dead shallow, look. I'm touching the bottom."

He was in already, splashing about and doing duck-dives. The pool was patched with cool shadow and an old willow leaned over it. Gillian felt envious; she could hardly swim, but she would have enjoyed this. Through the dappled water she could see bright pebbles patterning the bottom. It really wasn't very deep.

The main arm of the river was beyond the willow tree, on the other side of a kind of mud bank. The water had cut a channel through it and it was just wide enough to take Tom, if he did a glide, and kept still.

And suddenly Gillian went cold. He was swimming through the cut into the main river. It was only a grey flash of water through the branches but she could hear it, swollen by all the rain. "Tom!" she cried. "Come back! It'll be far too deep there, and the river's high. Remember what that man said. Don't be so silly!"

"Why don't you stop fussing?" Tom's voice came back confidently. "It's even shallower here, and I'm only on the edge. There's nothing to it."

But she was determined to get him out. She grabbed at overhead branches and hauled herself up the willow so she could see him. He was now several yards away from the bank, making for a line of big stones that reared up out of the water. He was doing a lot of splashing, and trying to speak.

"I told you, it's all right," she heard. But it was not. She could see that the water had already got hold of him, had snatched at his feet. He was at a bend in the stream where the land dropped suddenly down, and the water boiled and frothed over the stones. "Gill," he was calling, "Gill . . . I can't . . ." Then, "Get Dad!" in a muffled shout.

She watched the river take him and turn him over. He was so small. She thought there was blood on his face. He didn't seem to be moving down much, just thrashing his legs wildly, half on his back, trying to grab at a bit of fencing on the far bank that dipped into the water. She thought of that boy at their school who'd nearly drowned in a swimming-pool. She had seen the ambulance men take him away, his face green-white under the dark red stretcher blanket. That was why she was frightened of the water.

She tried to speak to Tom but no words would come out. It was as if all time had halted and the world was suddenly frozen, the trees, the sunlit river, the pink legs waving, and she was helpless with the horror of it.

Then something brushed past her face and she heard a strange, high crying. Through the grey-green willow branches she could see Tom jerking away from the big stones, trying to fling himself at the shattered piece of fencing that half floated out from the river bank. A great bird had covered the water with its wings and seemed to be wrenching something with its beak. She could see nothing clearly, only a flurry of pinkish feathers all mixed up with leaves and Tom's head and back, his fingers clawing at the fence-posts on the bank, where the river was lapping at the rusty barbed-wire turning the water a dirty red. She could see the small, bright eyes of the bird as it moved between the river and the land, tugging and straining, not letting go, uttering its shrill urgent cry.

"I'm here, don't worry," a voice said on the far side, and she saw somebody in a bright blue anorak leaning out towards Tom. "You his sister? Your dad's coming."

She must have been screaming. Suddenly the scene exploded round her head and she could hear her own voice in a tight shout, endlessly echoing down a long, long canyon, "Tom! Tom! Help him someone! Dad, where are you?" And almost at once her father was there, and Mum seemed to be crying, and somebody on the far side was helping the blue man wrap Tom in what looked like an enormous coat.

They had to spend the night in the village, at a pub called The Bear. The doctor came back to see Tom very early, before surgery, and told him to stick to swimming-pools in future. Then they sat over a large breakfast in almost total silence.

Mum and Dad had been arguing in their room about having left Tom with Gillian on the river bank, and she kept seeing his face under the water, and feeling sick. The only person not affected was Tom. He ate a hearty meal and started to talk loudly in the public dining-room, about what had happened, till Dad told him, icily, to keep quiet.

"It's a good thing those men were there," Mum said for about the twentieth time. "And that they got him to grab those posts. They knew what they were doing. He wasn't ever in any real danger." Gillian opened her mouth and shut it again. She knew. What point was there, now, in telling them what had really happened?

"I want to get in touch with them, to thank them properly," Dad said. "They were local, but they just pushed off when the doctor came. I could ask the vicar. He's still got my camera anyway."

Late in the morning they went back to the church to wait for him. "Funny," Dad said, after ten minutes. "He said he'd be here by twelve." Then they heard somebody walking up the path from the river. The vicar came through the gate in the wall, slowly, with something wrapped in a sack in his arms. He looked solemn.

"Sorry you've had to wait. Had rather a sad find this morning."

Gillian saw two spindly legs sticking out from the sacking, two yellowish feet, clumsily webbed. There was blood on the covering.

"It's Percy, isn't it?"

The vicar opened his eyes wide. "How on earth did you know that? It is, as a matter of fact. I was walking the dog this morning, early, and I spotted him in the water, just below the hermitage. He was all tangled up in some barbed-wire. Must have been out fishing, and got snarled up in it. Strange that, he knew this river so well. Looks as if it dragged him under the water, poor old chap. I had to go back for some wire cutters, to separate him from the fence. Vicious stuff, that wire is."

There was a silence. Then the vicar grinned and punched at Tom. "This young chap's all right, I see. That's marvellous. Enjoy the rest of your holiday, now. Oh, I'll just get the camera."

Gillian sat in the church under the pelican window. The angular, shiny glass bird feeding its young looked nothing like Percy. She stared sadly at the bright picture, seeing, instead, the large bird, pinky grey, staring solemnly out across the water like a stately sentinel, with the gentle northern hills behind.

They would never know where the bird had come from, the young man had told her, or why, so suddenly, it had decided to live by the river. But she knew now, and she gave thanks.

# THE ADVENTURES OF
# JOHNNIE WAVERLY
## AGATHA CHRISTIE

"YOU CAN UNDERSTAND the feelings of a mother," said Mrs Waverly for perhaps the sixth time. She looked appealingly at Poirot. My little friend, always sympathetic to motherhood in distress, gesticulated reassuringly

"But yes, but yes, I comprehend perfectly. Have faith in Papa Poirot."

"The police —" began Mr Waverly.

His wife waved the interruption aside. "I won't have anything more to do with the police. We trusted to them and look what happened! But I'd heard so much of M. Poirot and the wonderful things he'd done, that I felt he might possibly be able to help us. A mother's feelings —"

Poirot hastily stemmed the reiteration with an eloquent gesture. Mrs Waverly's emotion was obviously genuine, but it assorted strangely with her shrewd, rather hard type of countenance. When I heard later that she was the daughter of a prominent steel manufacturer who had worked his way up in the world from an office boy to his present eminence, I realized that she had inherited many of the paternal qualities.

Mr Waverly was a big, florid, jovial-looking man. He stood

with his legs straddled wide apart and looked the type of the country squire.

"I suppose you know all about this business, M. Poirot?"

The question was almost superfluous. For some days past the papers had been full of the sensational kidnapping of little Johnnie Waverly, the three-year-old son and heir of Marcus Waverly, Esq., of Waverly Court, Surrey, one of the oldest families in England.

"The main facts I know, of course, but recount to me the whole story, monsieur, I beg of you. And in detail if you please."

"Well, I suppose the beginning of the whole thing was about ten days ago when I got an anonymous letter – beastly things, anyway – that I couldn't make head or tail of. The writer had the impudence to demand that I should pay him twenty-five thousand pounds – twenty-five thousand pounds, M. Poirot! Failing my agreement, he threatened to kidnap Johnnie. Of course I threw the thing into the wastepaper basket without more ado. Thought it was some silly joke. Five days later I got another letter. 'Unless you pay, your son will be kidnapped on the twenty-ninth.' That was on the twenty-seventh. Ada was worried, but I couldn't bring myself to treat the matter seriously. Damn it all, we're in England. Nobody goes about kidnapping children and holding them up to ransom."

"It is not a common practice, certainly," said Poirot. "Proceed, monsieur."

"Well, Ada gave me no peace, so – feeling a bit of a fool –

I laid the matter before Scotland Yard. They didn't seem to take the thing very seriously – inclined to my view that it was some silly joke. On the twenty-eighth I got a third letter. 'You have not paid. Your son will be taken from you at twelve o'clock noon tomorrow, the twenty-ninth. It will cost you fifty thousand pounds to recover him.' Up I drove to Scotland Yard again. This time they were more impressed. They inclined to the view that the letters were written by a lunatic, and that in all probability an attempt of some kind would be made at the hour stated. They assured me that they would take all due precautions. Inspector McNeil and a sufficient force would come down to Waverly on the morrow and take charge.

"I went home much relieved in mind. Yet we already had the feeling of being in a state of siege. I gave orders that no stranger was to be admitted, and that no one was to leave the house. The evening passed off without any untoward incident, but on the following morning my wife was seriously unwell. Alarmed by her condition, I sent for Doctor Dakers. Her symptoms appeared to puzzle him. While hesitating to suggest that she had been poisoned, I could see that that was what was in his mind. There was no danger, he assured me, but it would be a day or two before she would be able to get about again. Returning to my own room, I was startled and amazed to find a note pinned to my pillow. It was in the same handwriting as the others and contained just three words: 'At twelve o'clock'.

"I admit, M. Poirot, that then I saw red! Someone in the house was in this – one of the servants. I had them all up, blackguarded them right and left. They never split on each other; it was Miss Collins, my wife's companion, who informed me that she had seen Johnnie's nurse slip down the drive early that morning. I taxed her with it, and she broke down. She had left the child with the nursery maid and stolen out to meet a friend of hers – a man! Pretty goings on! She denied having pinned the note to my pillow – she may have been speaking the truth, I don't know. I felt I couldn't take the risk of the child's own nurse being in the plot. One of the servants was implicated – of that I was sure. Finally I lost my temper and sacked the whole bunch, nurse and all. I gave them an hour to pack their boxes and get out of the house."

Mr Waverly's face was quite two shades redder as he remembered his just wrath.

"Was not that a little injudicious, monsieur?" suggested Poirot. "For all you know, you might have been playing into the enemy's hands."

Mr Waverly stared at him. "I don't see that. Send the whole lot packing, that was my idea. I wired to London for a fresh lot to be sent down that evening. In the meantime, there'd be only people I could trust in the house: my wife's secretary, Miss Collins, and Tredwell, the butler, who has been with me since I was a boy."

"And this Miss Collins, how long has she been with you?"

"Just a year," said Mrs Waverly. "She has been invaluable to me as a secretary-companion, and is also a very efficient housekeeper."

"The nurse?"

"She had been with me six months. She came to me with

excellent references. All the same, I never really liked her, although Johnnie was quite devoted to her."

"Still, I gather she had already left when the catastrophe occurred. Perhaps, Monsieur Waverly, you will be so kind as to continue."

Mr Waverly resumed his narrative.

"Inspector McNeil arrived about ten-thirty. The servants had all left by then. He declared himself quite satisfied with the internal arrangements. He had various men posted in the park outside, guarding all the approaches to the house, and he assured me that if the whole thing were not a hoax, we should undoubtedly catch my mysterious correspondent.

"I had Johnnie with me, and he and I and the inspector went together into the room we call the council chamber. The inspector locked the door. There is a big grandfather clock there, and as the hands drew near to twelve I don't mind confessing that I was as nervous as a cat. There was a whirring sound, and the clock began to strike. I clutched at Johnnie. I had a feeling a man might drop from the skies. The last stroke sounded, and as it did so, there was a great commotion outside – shouting and running. The inspector flung up the window, and a constable came running up.

"'We've got him sir,' he panted. 'He was sneaking up through the bushes. He's got a whole dope outfit on him.'

"We hurried out on the terrace where two constables were holding a ruffianly-looking fellow in shabby clothes, who was twisting and turning in a vain endeavour to escape. One of the policemen held out an unrolled parcel which they had wrested from their captive. It contained a pad of cotton wool and a bottle of chloroform. It made my blood boil to see it. There was a note, too, addressed to me. I tore it open. It bore the following words: 'You should have paid up. To ransom your son will now cost you fifty thousand. In spite of all your precautions he has been abducted on the twenty-ninth as I said.'

"I gave a great laugh, the laugh of relief, but as I did so I heard the hum of a motor and a shout. I turned my head. Racing down the drive towards the south lodge at a furious speed was a low, long grey car. It was the man who drove it who shouted, but that was not what gave me a shock of horror. It was the sight of Johnnie's flaxen curls. The child was in the car beside him.

"The inspector ripped out an oath. 'The child was here not a minute ago,' he cried. His eyes swept over us. We were all there: myself, Tredwell, Miss Collins. 'When did you last see him, Mr Waverly?'

"I cast my mind back, trying to remember. When the constable had called us, I had run out with the inspector, forgetting all about Johnnie.

"And then there came a sound that startled us, the chiming of a church clock from the village. With an exclamation the inspector pulled out his watch. It was exactly twelve o'clock. With one common accord we ran to the council chamber; the clock there marked the hour as ten minutes past. Someone must have deliberately tampered with it, for I have never known it gain or lose before. It is a perfect timekeeper."

Mr Waverly paused. Poirot smiled to himself and straightened a little mat which the anxious father had pushed askew.

"A pleasing little problem, obscure and charming," murmured Poirot. "I will investigate it for you with pleasure. Truly it was planned *à merveille*."

Mrs Waverly looked at him reproachfully. "But my boy," she wailed.

Poirot hastily composed his face and looked the picture of earnest sympathy again. "He is safe, madame, he is unharmed. Rest assured, these miscreants will take the greatest care of him. Is he not to them the turkey – no, the goose – that lays the golden eggs?"

"M. Poirot, I'm sure there's only one thing to be done – pay up. I was all against it at first – but now! A mother's feelings —"

"But we have interrupted monsieur in his history," cried Poirot hastily.

"I expect you know the rest pretty well from the papers," said Mr Waverly. "Of course, Inspector McNeil got on to the telephone immediately. A description of the car and the man was circulated all round, and it looked at first as though everything was going to turn out all right. A car answering to the description, with a man and a small boy, had passed through various villages, apparently making for London. At one place they had stopped, and it was noticed that the child was crying and obviously afraid of his companion. When Inspector McNeil announced that the car had been stopped and the man and boy detained, I was almost ill with relief. You know the sequel. The boy was not Johnnie, and the man was an ardent motorist, fond of children, who had picked up a small child playing in the streets of Edenswell, a village about fifteen miles from us, and was kindly giving him a ride. Thanks to the cocksure blundering of the police, all traces have disappeared. Had they not persistently followed the wrong car, they might by now have found the boy."

"Calm yourself, monsieur. The police are a brave and intelligent force of men. Their mistake was a very natural one. And altogether it was a clever scheme. As to the man they caught in the grounds, I understand that his defence has consisted all along of a persistent denial. He declared that the note and parcel were given to him to deliver at Waverly Court. The man who gave them to him handed him a ten-shilling note and promised him another if it were delivered at exactly ten minutes to twelve. He was to approach the house through the grounds and knock at the side door."

"I don't believe a word of it," declared Mrs Waverly hotly. "It's all a parcel of lies."

"*En verité*, it is a thin story," said Poirot reflectively. "But so far they have not shaken it. I understand, also, that he made a certain accusation?"

His glance interrogated Mr Waverly. The latter got rather red again.

"The fellow had the impertinence to pretend that he recognized in Tredwell the man who gave him the parcel. 'Only the bloke has shaved off his moustache.' Tredwell, who was born on the estate!"

Poirot smiled a little at the country gentleman's indignation. "Yet you yourself suspect an inmate of the house to have been accessory to the abduction."

"Yes, but not Tredwell."

"And you, madame?" asked Poirot, suddenly turning to her.

"It could not have been Tredwell who gave this tramp the letter and parcel – if anybody ever did, which I don't believe. It was given him at ten o'clock, he says. At ten o'clock Tredwell was with my husband in the smoking-room."

"Were you able to see the face of the man in the car, monsieur? Did it resemble that of Tredwell in any way?"

"It was too far away for me to see his face."

"Has Tredwell a brother, do you know?"

"He had several, but they are all dead. The last one was killed in the war."

"I am not yet clear as to the grounds of Waverly Court. The car was heading for the south lodge. Is there another entrance?"

"Yes, what we call the east lodge. It can be seen from the other side of the house."

"It seems to me strange that nobody saw the car entering the grounds."

"There is a right of way through, and access to a small chapel. A good many cars pass through. The man must have stopped the car in a convenient place and run up to the house just as the alarm was given and attention attracted elsewhere."

"Unless he was already inside the house," mused Poirot. "Is

there any place where he could have hidden?"

"Well, we certainly didn't make a thorough search of the house beforehand. There seemed no need. I suppose he might have hidden himself somewhere, but who would have let him in?"

"We shall come to that later. One thing at a time – let us be methodical. There is no special hiding-place in the house? Waverly Court is an old place, and there are sometimes 'priests' holes', as they call them."

"By gad, there *is* a priest's hole. It opens from one of the panels in the hall."

"Near the council chamber?"

"Just outside the door."

"*Voilà!*"

"But nobody knows of its existence except my wife and myself."

"Tredwell?"

"Well – he might have heard of it."

"Miss Collins?"

"I have never mentioned it to her."

Poirot reflected for a minute.

"Well, monsieur, the next thing is for me to come down to Waverly Court. If I arrive this afternoon, will it suit you?"

"Oh, as soon as possible, please, Monsieur Poirot!" cried Mrs Waverly. "Read this once more."

She thrust into his hands the last missive from the enemy which had reached the Waverlys that morning and which had sent her post-haste to Poirot. It gave clever and explicit directions for the paying over of the money, and ended with a threat that the boy's life would pay for any treachery. It was clear that a love of money warred with the essential mother love of Mrs Waverly, and that the latter was at last gaining the day.

Poirot detained Mrs Waverly for a minute behind her husband.

"Madame, the truth, if you please. Do you share your husband's faith in the butler, Tredwell?"

"I have nothing against him, Monsieur Poirot, I cannot see how he can have been concerned in this, but – well, I have never liked him – never!"

"One other thing, Madame, can you give me the address of the child's nurse?"

"149 Netherall Road, Hammersmith. You don't imagine —"

"Never do I imagine. Only – I employ the little grey cells. And sometimes, just sometimes, I have a little idea."

Poirot came back to me as the door closed.

"So madame has never liked the butler. It is interesting, that, eh, Hastings?"

I refused to be drawn. Poirot has deceived me so often that I now go warily. There is always a catch somewhere.

After completing an elaborate outdoor toilet, we set off for Netherall Road. We were fortunate enough to find Miss Jessie Withers at home. She was a pleasant-faced woman of thirty-five, capable and superior. I could not believe that she could be mixed up in the affair. She was bitterly resentful of the way she had been dismissed, but admitted that she had been in the wrong. She was engaged to be married to a painter and decorator who happened to be in the neighbourhood, and she had run out to meet him. The thing seemed natural enough. I could not quite understand Poirot. All his questions seemed to me quite irrelevant. They were concerned mainly with the daily routine of her life at Waverly Court. I was frankly bored and glad when Poirot took his departure.

"Kidnapping is an easy job, *mon ami*," he observed, as he hailed a taxi in the Hammersmith Road and ordered it to drive to Waterloo. "That child could have been abducted with the greatest ease any day for the last three years."

"I don't see that that advances us much," I remarked coldly.

"*Au contraire*, it advances us enormously, but enormously! If you must wear a tie pin, Hastings, at least let it be in the exact centre of your tie. At present it is at least a sixteenth of an inch too much to the right."

Waverly Court was a fine old place and had recently been restored with taste and care. Mr Waverly showed us the council chamber, the terrace, and all the various spots connected with the case. Finally, at Poirot's request, he pressed a spring in the wall, a panel slid aside, and a short passage led us into the priest's hole.

"You see," said Waverly. "There is nothing here."

The tiny room was bare enough, there was not even the mark of a footstep on the floor. I joined Poirot where he was bending attentively over a mark in the corner.

"What do you make of this, my friend?"

There were four imprints close together.

"A dog," I cried.

"A very small dog, Hastings."

"A Pom."

"Smaller than a Pom."

"A griffon?" I suggested doubtfully.

"Smaller even than a griffon. A species unknown to the Kennel Club."

I looked at him. His face was alight with excitement and satisfaction.

"I was right," he murmured. "I knew I was right. Come, Hastings."

As we stepped out into the hall and the panel closed behind us, a young lady came out of a door farther down the passage. Mr Waverly presented her to us.

"Miss Collins."

Miss Collins was about thirty years of age, brisk and alert in manner. She had fair, rather dull hair, and wore pince-nez.

At Poirot's request, we passed into a small morning-room, and he questioned her closely as to the servants and particularly as to Tredwell. She admitted that she did not like the butler.

"He gives himself airs," she explained.

They then went into the question of the food eaten by Mrs Waverly on the night of the twenty-eighth. Miss Collins declared that she had partaken of the same dishes upstairs in her sitting-room and had felt no ill effects. As she was departing I nudged Poirot.

"The dog," I whispered.

"Ah, yes, the dog!" He smiled broadly. "Is there a dog kept here by any chance, mademoiselle?"

"There are two retrievers in the kennels outside."

"No, I mean a small dog, a toy dog."

"No – nothing of the kind."

Poirot permitted her to depart. Then, pressing the bell, he remarked to me, "She lies, that Mademoiselle Collins. Possibly I should, also, in her place. Now for the butler."

Tredwell was a dignified individual. He told his story with perfect aplomb, and it was essentially the same as that of Mr Waverly. He admitted that he knew the secret of the priest's hole.

When he finally withdrew, pontifical to the last, I met Poirot's quizzical eyes.

"What do you make of it all, Hastings?"

"What do you?" I parried.

"How cautious you become. Never, never will the grey cells function unless you stimulate them. Ah, but I will not tease you! Let us make our deductions together. What points strike us specially as being difficult?"

"There is one thing that strikes me," I said. "Why did the man who kidnapped the child go out by the south lodge instead of by the east lodge where no one would see him?"

"That is a very good point, Hastings, an excellent one. I will match it with another. Why warn the Waverlys beforehand? Why not simply kidnap the child and hold him to ransom?"

"Because they hoped to get the money without being forced to action."

"Surely it was very unlikely that the money would be paid on a mere threat?"

"Also they wanted to focus attention on twelve o'clock, so that when the tramp man was seized, the other could emerge from his hiding-place and get away with the child unnoticed."

"That does not alter the fact that they were making a thing difficult that was perfectly easy. If they do not specify a time or date, nothing would be easier than to wait their chance, and carry off the child in a motor one day when he is out with his nurse."

"Y—es," I admitted doubtfully.

"In fact, there is a deliberate playing of the farce! Now let us approach the question from another side. Everything goes to show that there was an accomplice inside the house. Point number one, the mysterious poisoning of Mrs Waverly. Point number two, the letter pinned to the pillow. Point number three, the putting on of the clock ten minutes – all inside jobs. And an additional fact that you may not have noticed. There was no dust in the priest's hole. It had been swept out with a broom.

"Now then, we have four people in the house. We can exclude the nurse, since she could not have swept out the priest's hole, though she could have attended to the other three points. Four people, Mr and Mrs Waverly, Tredwell, the butler, and Miss Collins. We will take Miss Collins first. We have nothing much against her, except that we know very little about her, that she is obviously an intelligent young woman, and that she has only been here a year."

"She lied about the dog, you said," I reminded him.

"Ah, yes, the dog." Poirot gave a peculiar smile. "Now let us pass to Tredwell. There are several suspicious facts against him. For one thing, the tramp declares that it was Tredwell who gave him the parcel in the village."

"But Tredwell can prove an alibi on that point."

"Even then, he could have poisoned Mrs Waverly, pinned the note to the pillow, put on the clock, and swept out the priest's hole. On the other hand, he has been born and bred in the service of the Waverlys. It seems unlikely in the last degree that he should connive at the abduction of the son of the house. It is not in the picture!"

"Well, then?"

"We must proceed logically – however absurd it may seem. We will briefly consider Mrs Waverly. But she is rich, the money is hers. It is her money which has restored this impoverished estate. There would be no reason for her to kidnap her son and pay over her money to herself. The husband, no, is in a different position. He has a rich wife. It is not the same thing as being rich himself – in fact I have a little idea that the lady is not very fond of parting with her money, except on a very good pretext. But Mr Waverly, you can see at once, he is a *bon viveur.*"

"Impossible," I spluttered.

"Not at all. Who sends away the servants? Mr Waverly. He can write the notes, drug his wife, put on the hands of the clock, and establish an excellent alibi for his faithful retainer Tredwell. Tredwell has never liked Mrs Waverly. He is devoted to his master and is willing to obey his orders implicitly. There were three of them in it. Waverly, Tredwell, and some friend of Waverly. That is the mistake the police made, they made no further inquiries about the man who drove the grey car with the wrong child in it. He was the third man. He picks up a child in a village near by, a boy with flaxen curls. He drives in through the east lodge and passes out through the south lodge just at the right moment, waving his hand and shouting. They cannot see his face or the number of the car, so obviously they cannot see the child's face, either. Then he lays a false trail to London. In the meantime, Tredwell has done his part in arranging for the parcel and note to be delivered by a rough-looking gentleman. His master can provide an alibi in the unlikely case of the man recognizing him, in spite of the false moustache he wore. As for Mr Waverly, as soon as the hullabaloo occurs outside, and the inspector rushes out, he quickly hides the child in the priest's hole, follows him out. Later in the day, when the inspector is gone and Miss Collins is out of the way, it will be easy enough to drive him off to some safe place in his own car."

"But what about the dog?" I asked. "And Miss Collins lying?"

"That was my little joke. I asked her if there were any toy dogs in the house, and she said no – but doubtless there are some – in the nursery! You see, Mr Waverly placed some toys in the priest's hole to keep Johnnie amused and quiet."

"M. Poirot —" Mr Waverly entered the room — "have you discovered anything? Have you any clue to where the boy has been taken?"

Poirot handed him a piece of paper. "Here is the address."

"But this is a blank sheet."

"Because I am waiting for you to write it down for me."

"What the —" Mr Waverly's face turned purple.

"I know everything, monsieur. I give you twenty-four hours to return the boy. Your ingenuity will be equal to the task of explaining his reappearance. Otherwise, Mrs Waverly will be informed of the exact sequence of events."

Mr Waverly sank down in a chair and buried his face in his hands. "He is with my old nurse, ten miles away. He is happy and well cared for."

"I have no doubt of that. If I did not believe you to be a good father at heart, I should not be willing to give you another chance."

"The scandal —"

"Exactly. Your name is an old and honoured one. Do not jeopardize it again. Good evening, Mr Waverly. Ah, by the way, one word of advice. Always sweep in the corners!"

# THE TOWER
## CARL JUNG

*In his eighty-third year the great psychologist C. G. Jung wrote his life story,* Memories, Dreams, Reflections. *This is not an autobiography in the ordinary sense, because he was not interested in the outer events of his life. In his Preface he says "In the end the only events in my life worth telling are those when the imperishable world irrupted into this transitory one. That is why I speak chiefly of inner experiences, amongst which I include my dreams and visions." This is his account of one such experience at Bollingen, a remote place where he built for himself a house, with a tower where he could be alone.*

I WAS IN Bollingen just as the first tower was being finished. This was the winter of 1923–24. As far as I can recall, there was no snow on the ground; perhaps it was early spring. I had been alone perhaps for a week, perhaps longer. An indescribable stillness prevailed.

One evening – I can still remember it precisely – I was sitting by the fireplace and had put a big kettle on the fire to make hot water for washing up. The water began to boil and the kettle to sing. It sounded like many voices, or stringed instruments, or even like a whole orchestra. It was just like polyphonic music, which in reality I cannot abide, though in this case it seemed to me peculiarly interesting. It was as though there were one orchestra inside the Tower and another one outside. Now one dominated, now the other, as though they were responding to each other.

I sat and listened, fascinated. For far more than an hour I listened to the concert, to this natural melody. It was soft music, containing, as well, all the discords of nature. And that was right, for nature is not only harmonious; she is also dreadfully contradictory and chaotic. The music was that way too: an outpouring of sounds, having the quality of water and of wind – so strange that it is simply impossible to describe it.

On another such still night when I was alone in Bollingen (it was in the late winter or early spring of 1924) I awoke to the sound of soft footsteps going round the Tower. Distant music sounded, coming closer and closer, and then I heard voices laughing and talking. I thought, *Who can be prowling around? What is this all about? There is only the little footpath along the lake, and scarcely anybody ever walks on it!* While I was thinking these things I became wide awake, and went to the window. I opened the shutters – all was still. There was no one in sight, nothing to be heard – no wind – nothing – nothing at all.

*This is really strange*, I thought. I was certain that the footsteps, and laughter and talk, had been real. But apparently I had only been dreaming. I returned to bed and mulled over the way we can deceive ourselves after all, and what might have been the cause of such a strange dream. In the midst of all this, I fell asleep again – and at once the same dream began: once more I heard footsteps, talk, laughter, music. At the same time I had a visual image of several hundred dark-clad figures, possibly peasant boys in their Sunday clothes, who had come down from the mountains and were pouring in around the Tower, on both sides, with a great deal of loud trampling, laughing, singing, and playing of accordions. Irritably, I thought, *This is really the limit! I thought it was a dream and now it turns out to be reality!* At this point, I woke up. Once again I jumped up, opened the window and shutters, and found everything just the same as before: a deathly still moonlit night. Then I thought: *Why, this is simply a case of haunting!*

Naturally I asked myself what it meant when a dream was so insistent on its reality and at the same time on my being awake. Usually we experience that only when we see a ghost. Being awake means perceiving reality. The dream therefore represented a situation equivalent to reality, in which it created a kind of wakened state. In this sort of dream, as opposed to ordinary dreams, the unconscious seems bent on conveying a powerful impression of reality to the dreamer, an impression which is emphasized by repetition. The sources of such realities are known to be physical sensations on the one hand, and archetypal figures on the other.

That night everything was so completely real, or at least seemed to be so, that I could scarcely sort out the two realities. Nor could I make anything of the dream itself. What was the meaning of these music-making peasant boys passing by in a long procession? It seemed to me they had come out of curiosity, in order to look at the Tower.

Never again did I experience or dream anything similar, and I cannot recall ever having heard of a parallel to it. It was only much later that I found an explanation. This was when I came across the seventeenth-century Lucerne chronicle by Rennward Cysat. He tells the following story: on a high pasture of Mount Pilatus, which is particularly notorious for apparitions – it is said that Wotan to this day practises his magic arts there – Cysat, while climbing the mountain, was disturbed one night by a procession of men who poured past his hut on both sides, playing music and singing – precisely what I had experienced at the Tower.

The next morning Cysat asked the herdsman with whom he had spent that night what could have been the meaning of it. The man had a ready explanation: those must be the departed folk – *sälig Lüt* in Swiss dialect; the phrase also means blessed folk – namely, Wotan's army of departed souls. These, he said, were in the habit of walking abroad and showing themselves.

It may be suggested that this is a phenomenon of solitude, the outward emptiness and silence being compensated by the image of a crowd of people. This would put it in the same class with the hallucinations of hermits, which are likewise compensatory. But do we know what realities such stories may be founded on? It is also possible that I had been so sensitized by the solitude that I was able to perceive the procession of "departed folk" who passed by.

The explanation of this experience as a psychic compensation never entirely satisfied me, and to say that it was a hallucination seemed to me to beg the question. I felt obliged to consider the possibility of its reality, especially in view of the seventeenth-century account which had come my way.

It would seem most likely to have been a synchronistic phenomenon. Such phenomena demonstrate that premonitions or visions very often have some correspondence in external reality. There actually existed, as I discovered, a real parallel to my experience. In the Middle Ages just such gatherings of young men took place. These were the *Reislaüfer* (mercenaries) who usually assembled in spring, marched from central Switzerland to Locarno, met at the Casa di Ferro in Minusio and then marched on together to Milan. In Italy they served as soldiers, fighting for foreign princes. My visions, therefore, might have been one of these gatherings which took place regularly each spring when the young men, with singing and jollity, bade farewell to their native land.

# THE SCYTHE
## RAY BRADBURY

QUITE SUDDENLY THERE was no more road. It ran down the valley like any other road, between slopes of barren, stony ground and live oak trees, and then past a broad field of wheat standing alone in the wilderness. It came up beside the small white house that belonged to the wheat field and then just faded out, as though there was no more use for it.

It didn't matter much, because just there the last of the gas was gone. Drew Erickson braked the ancient car to a stop and sat there, not speaking, staring at his big, rough farmer's hands.

Molly spoke, without moving where she lay in the corner beside him. "We must of took the wrong fork back yonder."

Drew nodded.

Molly's lips were almost as white as her face. Only they were dry, where her skin was damp with sweat. Her voice was flat, with no expression in it.

"Drew," she said. "Drew, what are we a-goin' to do now?"

Drew stared at his hands. A farmer's hands, with the farm blown out from under them by the dry, hungry wind that never got enough good loam to eat.

The kids in the back seat woke up and pried themselves

out of the dusty litter of bundles and bedding. They poked their heads over the back of the seat and said, "What are we stoppin' for, Pa? Are we gonna eat now, Pa? Pa, we're awful hungry. Can we eat now, Pa?"

Drew closed his eyes. He hated the sight of his hands.

Molly's fingers touched his wrist. Very light, very soft. "Drew, maybe in the house there they'd spare us somethin' to eat?"

A white line showed around his mouth. "Beggin'," he said harshly. "Ain't none of us ever begged before. Ain't none of us ever goin' to."

Molly's hand tightened on his wrist. He turned and saw her eyes. He saw the eyes of Susie and little Drew, looking at him. Slowly all the stiffness went out of his neck and his back. His face got loose and blank, shapeless like a thing that has been beaten too hard and too long. He got out of the car and went up the path to the house. He walked uncertainly, like a man who is sick, or nearly blind.

The door of the house was open. Drew knocked three times. There was nothing inside but silence, and a white window curtain moving in the slow, hot air.

He knew it before he went in. He knew there was death in the house. It was that kind of silence.

He went through a small, clean living-room and down a little hall. He wasn't thinking anything. He was past thinking. He was going towards the kitchen, unquestioning, like an animal.

Then he looked through an open door and saw the dead man.

# THE SCYTHE

He was an old man, lying out on a clean white bed. He hadn't been dead long; not long enough to lose the last quiet look of peace. He must have known he was going to die, because he wore his grave clothes – an old black suit, brushed and neat, and a clean white shirt and a black tie.

A scythe leaned against the wall beside the bed. Between the old man's hands there was a blade of wheat, still fresh. A ripe blade, golden and heavy in the tassel.

Drew went into the bedroom, walking soft. There was a coldness on him. He took off his broken, dusty hat and stood by the bed, looking down.

The paper lay open on the pillow beside the old man's head. It was meant to be read. Maybe a request for burial, or to call a relative. Drew scowled over the words, moving his pale, dry lips.

*To him who stands beside me at my death bed:* Being of sound mind, and alone in the world as it has been decreed, I, John Buhr, do give and bequeath this farm, with all pertaining to it, to the man who is to come. Whatever his name or origin shall be, it will not matter. The farm is his, and the wheat; the scythe, and the task ordained thereto. Let him take them freely, and without question – and remember that I, John Buhr, am only the giver, not the ordainer. To which I set my hand and seal this third day of April, 1938. (Signed) John Buhr. *Kyrie eleison!*

Drew walked back through the house and opened the screen door. He said, "Molly, you come in. Kids, you stay in the car."

Molly came inside. He took her to the bedroom. She looked at the will, the scythe, the wheat field moving in a hot wind outside the window. Her white face tightened up and she bit her lips and held onto him. "It's too good to be true. There must be some trick to it."

Drew said, "Our luck's changin', that's all. We'll have work to do, stuff to eat, somethin' over our heads to keep rain off." He touched the scythe. It gleamed like a half-moon. Words were scratched on its blade: WHO WIELDS ME – WIELDS THE WORLD! It didn't mean much to him, right at that moment.

"Drew," Molly asked, staring at the old man's clasped hands, "why – why's he holdin' that wheat-stalk so hard in his fingers?"

Just then the heavy silence was broken by the sound of the kids scrambling up the front porch. Molly gasped.

They lived in the house. They buried the old man on a hill and said some words over him, and came back down and swept the house and unloaded the car and had something to eat, because there was food, lots of it, in the kitchen; and they did nothing for three days but fix the house and look at the land and lie in the good beds, and then look at one another in surprise that all this was happening in this way, and their stomachs were full and there was even a cigar for him to smoke in the evenings.

There was a small barn behind the house and in the barn a bull and three cows; and there was a well-house, a spring-house, under some big trees that kept cool. And inside the well-house were big sides of beef and bacon and pork and mutton, enough to feed a family five times their size for a year, two years, maybe three. There was a churn and a box of cheese there, and big metal cans for the milk.

On the fourth morning Drew Erickson lay in bed looking at the scythe, and he knew it was time for him to work because there was ripe grain in the long field; he had seen it with his eyes, and he did not want to get soft. Three days sitting were enough for any man. He roused himself in the first fresh smell of dawn and took the scythe and held it before him as he walked out into the field. He held it up in his hands and swung it down.

It was a big field of grain. Too big for one man to tend, and yet one man had tended it.

At the end of the first day of work, he walked in with the scythe riding his shoulder quietly, and there was a look on his face of a puzzled man. It was a wheat field the like of which he had never seen. It ripened only in separate clusters, each set off from the others. Wheat shouldn't do that. He didn't tell Molly. Nor did he tell her the other things about the field. About how, for instance, the wheat rotted within a few hours after he cut it down. Wheat shouldn't do that, either. He was not greatly worried. After all, there was food at hand.

The next morning the wheat he had left rotting, cut down, had taken hold and came up again in little green sprouts, with tiny roots, all born again.

Drew Erickson rubbed his chin, wondered what and why and how it acted that way, and what good it would be to him

− he couldn't sell it. A couple of times during the day he walked far up in the hills to where the old man's grave was, just to be sure the old man was there, maybe with some notion he might get an idea there about the field. He looked down and saw how much land he owned. The wheat stretched three miles in one direction toward the mountains, and was about two acres wide, patches of it in seedlings, patches of it golden, patches of it green, patches of it fresh cut by his hand. But the old man said nothing concerning this; there were a lot of stones and dirt in his face now. The grave was in the sun and the wind and silence. So Drew Erickson walked back down to use the scythe, curious, enjoying it because it seemed important. He didn't know just why, but it was. Very, very important.

He couldn't just let the wheat stand. There were always new patches of it ripened, and in his figuring out loud to no one in particular he said, "If I cut the wheat for the next ten years, just as it ripens up, I don't think I'll pass the same spot twice. Such a damn big field." He shook his head. "That wheat ripens just so. Never too much of it so I can't cut all the ripe stuff each day. That leaves nothin' but green grain. And the next mornin', sure enough, another patch of ripe stuff . . ."

It was damned foolish to cut the grain when it rotted as quick as it fell. At the end of the week he decided to let it go a few days.

He lay in bed late, just listening to the silence in the house that wasn't anything like death silence, but a silence of things living well and happily.

He got up, dressed, and ate his breakfast slowly. He wasn't going to work. He went out to milk the cows, stood on the porch smoking a cigarette, walked about the backyard a little and then came back in and asked Molly what he had gone out to do.

"Milk the cows," she said.

"Oh, yes," he said, and went out again. He found the cows waiting and full, and milked them and put the milk cans in the spring-house, but thought of other things. The wheat. The scythe.

All through the morning he sat on the back porch rolling cigarettes. He made a toy boat for little Drew and one for Susie, and then he churned some of the milk into butter and drew off the buttermilk, but the sun was in his head, aching. It burned there. He wasn't hungry for lunch. He kept looking at the wheat and wind bending and tipping and ruffling it. His arms flexed, his fingers, resting on his knee as he sat again on the porch, made a kind of grip in the empty air, itching. The pads of his palms itched and burned. He stood up and wiped his hands on his pants and sat down and tried to roll another cigarette and got mad at the mixings and threw it all away with a muttering. He had a feeling as if a third arm had been cut off of him, or he had lost something of himself. It had to do with his hands and his arms.

He heard the wind whisper in the field.

By one o'clock he was going in and out of the house, getting underfoot, thinking about digging an irrigation ditch, but all the time really thinking about the wheat and how ripe and beautiful it was, aching to be cut.

"Damn it to hell!"

He strode into the bedroom, took the scythe down off its wall-pegs. He stood holding it. He felt cool. His hands stopped itching. His head didn't ache. The third arm was returned to him. He was intact again.

It was instinct. Illogical as lightning striking and not hurting. Each day the grain must be cut. It had to be cut. Why? Well, it just did, that was all. He laughed at the scythe in his big hands. Then, whistling, he took it out to the ripe and waiting field and did the work. He thought himself a little mad. Hell, it was an ordinary-enough wheat field, really, wasn't it? Almost.

The days loped away like gentle horses.

Drew Erickson began to understand his work as a sort of dry ache and hunger and need. Things built in his head.

One noon, Susie and little Drew giggled and played with the scythe while their father lunched in the kitchen. He heard them. He came out and took it away from them. He didn't yell at them. He just looked very concerned and locked the scythe up after that, when it wasn't being used.

He never missed a day, scything.

Up. Down. Up, down and across. Back up and down and across. Cutting. Up. Down.

Up.

Think about the old man and the wheat in his hands when he died.

Down.

# THE SCYTHE

Think about this dead land, with wheat living on it.

Up.

Think about the crazy patterns of ripe and green wheat, the way it grows!

Down.

Think about . . .

The wheat whirled in a full yellow tide at his ankles. The sky blackened. Drew Erickson dropped the scythe and bent over to hold his stomach, his eyes running blindly. The world reeled.

"I've killed somebody!" he gasped, choking, holding to his chest, falling to his knees beside the blade. "I've killed a lot –"

The sky revolved like a blue merry-go-round at the county fair in Kansas. But no music. Only a ringing in his ears.

Molly was sitting at the blue kitchen table peeling potatoes when he blundered into the kitchen, dragging the scythe behind him.

"Molly!"

She swam around in the wet of his eyes.

She sat there, her hands fallen open, waiting for him to finally get it out.

"Get the things packed!" he said, looking at the floor.

"Why?"

"We're leaving," he said, dully.

"We're leaving?" she said.

"That old man. You know what he did here? It's the wheat, Molly, and this scythe. Every time you use the scythe on the wheat a thousand people die. You cut across them and —"

Molly got up and put the knife down and the potatoes to one side and said, understandingly, "We travelled a lot and haven't eaten good until the last month here, and you been workin' every day and you're tired —"

"I hear voices, sad voices, out there. In the wheat," he said. "Tellin' me to stop. Tellin' me not to kill them!"

"Drew!"

He didn't hear her. "The field grows crooked, wild, like a crazy thing. I didn't tell you. But it's wrong."

She stared at him. His eyes were blue glass, nothing else.

"You think I'm crazy," he said, "but wait 'til I tell you. Oh, God, Molly, help me; I just killed my mother!"

"Stop it!" she said firmly.

"I cut down one stalk of wheat and I killed her. I felt her dyin', that's how I found out just now —"

"Drew!" Her voice was like a crack across the face, angry and afraid now. "Shut up!"

He mumbled. "Oh – Molly —"

The scythe dropped from his hands, clamoured on the floor. She picked it up with a snap of anger and set it in one corner. "Ten years I been with you," she said. "Sometimes we had nothin' but dust and prayers in our mouths. Now, all this good luck sudden, and you can't bear up under it!"

She brought the Bible from the living-room.

She rustled its pages over. They sounded like the wheat rustling in a small slow wind. "You sit down and listen," she said.

A sound came in from the sunshine. The kids, laughing in

the shade of the large live oak beside the house.

She read from the Bible, looking up now and again to see what was happening to Drew's face.

She read from the Bible each day after that. The following Wednesday, a week later, when Drew walked down to the distant town to see if there was any General Delivery mail, there was a letter.

He came home looking two hundred years old.

He held the letter out to Molly and told her what it said in a cold, uneven voice.

"Mother passed away – one o'clock Tuesday afternoon – her heart —"

All that Drew Erickson had to say was, "Get the kids in the car, load it up with food. We're goin' to California."

"Drew —" said his wife, holding the letter.

"You know yourself," he said, "this is poor grain land. Yet look how ripe it grows. I ain't told you all the things. It ripens in patches, a little each day. It ain't right. And when I cut it, it rots! And next mornin' it comes up without any help, growin' again! Last Tuesday, a week ago, when I cut the grain it was like rippin' my own flesh. I heard somebody scream. It sounded just like – And now, today, this letter."

She said, "We're stayin' here."

"Molly."

"We're stayin' here, where we're sure of eatin' and sleepin' and livin' decent and livin' long. I'm not starvin' my children down again, ever!"

The sky was blue through the windows. The sun slanted in,

touching half of Molly's calm face, shining one eye bright blue. Four or five water drops hung and fell from the kitchen faucet slowly, shining, before Drew sighed. The sigh was husky and resigned and tired. He nodded, looking away. "All right," he said. "We'll stay."

He picked up the scythe weakly. The words on the metal leaped up with a sharp glitter.

WHO WIELDS ME – WIELDS THE WORLD!

"We'll stay . . ."

Next morning he walked to the old man's grave. There was a single fresh sprout of wheat growing in the centre of it. The same sprout, reborn, that the old man had held in his hands weeks before.

He talked to the old man, getting no answers.

"You worked the field all your life because you *had* to, and one day you came across your own life growin' there. You knew it was yours. You cut it. And you went home, put on your grave clothes, and your heart gave out and you died. That's how it was, wasn't it? And you passed the land on to me, and when I die, I'm supposed to hand it over to someone else."

Drew's voice had awe in it. "How long a time has this been goin' on? With nobody knowin' about this field and its use except the man with the scythe . . .?"

Quite suddenly he felt very old. The valley seemed ancient, mummified, secretive, dried and bent and powerful. When the Indians danced on the prairie it had been here, this field. The same sky, the same wind, the same wheat. And, before the

Indians? Some Cro-Magnon, gnarled and shag-haired, wielding a crude wooden scythe, perhaps, prowling down through the living wheat . . .

Drew returned to work. Up, down. Up, down. Obsessed with the idea of being the wielder of *the* scythe. He, himself! It burst upon him in a mad, wild surge of strength and horror.

Up! WHO WIELDS ME! Down! WIELDS THE WORLD!

He had to accept the job with some sort of philosophy. It was simply his way of getting food and housing for his family. They deserved eating and living decent, he thought, after all these years.

Up and down. Each grain a life he neatly cut into two pieces. If he planned it carefully – he looked at the wheat – why, he and Molly and the kids could live forever!

Once he found the place where the grain grew that was Molly and Susie and little Drew he would never cut it.

And then, like a signal, it came, quietly.

Right there, before him.

Another sweep of the scythe and he'd cut them away.

Molly, Drew, Susie. It was certain. Trembling, he knelt and looked at the few grains of wheat. They glowed at his touch.

He groaned with relief. What if he had cut them down, never guessing? He blew out his breath and got up and took the scythe and stood back away from the wheat and stood for a long time while looking down.

Molly thought it awfully strange when he came home early and kissed her on the cheek, for no reason at all.

At dinner, Molly said, "You quit early today? Does – does the wheat still spoil when it falls?"

He nodded and took more meat.

She said, "You ought to write to the Agriculture people and have them come look at it."

"No," he said.

"I was just suggestin'," she said.

His eyes dilated. "I got to stay here all my life. Can't nobody else mess with that wheat; they wouldn't know where to cut and not to cut. They might cut the wrong parts."

"What wrong parts?"

"Nothin'," he said, chewing slowly. "Nothin' at all."

He slapped his fork down, hard. "Who knows *what* they might want to do! Those government men! They might even – might even want to plough the whole field under!"

Molly nodded. "That's just what it needs," she said.

"And start all over again, with new seed."

He didn't finish eating. "I'm not writin' any gover'ment, and I'm not handin' this field over to no stranger to cut, and that's that!" he said, and the screen door banged behind him.

He detoured around that place where the lives of his children and his wife grew up in the sun, and used his scythe on the far end of the field where he knew he would make no mistakes.

But he no longer liked the work. At the end of an hour he knew he had brought death to three of his old, loved friends in Missouri. He read their names in the cut grain and couldn't go on.

# THE SCYTHE

He locked the scythe in the cellar and put the key away. He was done with the reaping, done for good and all.

He smoked his pipe in the evening, on the front porch, and told the kids stories to hear them laugh. But they didn't laugh much. They seemed withdrawn, tired and funny, like they weren't his children any more.

Molly complained of a headache, dragged around the house a little, went to bed early and fell into a deep sleep. That was funny, too. Molly always stayed up late and was full of vinegar.

The wheat field rippled with moonlight on it, making it into a sea.

It wanted cutting. Certain parts needed cutting *now*. Drew Erickson sat, swallowing quietly, trying not to look at it.

What'd happen to the world if he never went in the field again? What'd happen to people ripe for death, who waited the coming of the scythe?

He'd wait and see.

Molly was breathing softly when he blew out the oil lamp and got to bed. He couldn't sleep. He heard the wind in the wheat, felt the hunger to do the work in his arms and fingers.

In the middle of the night he found himself walking in the field, the scythe in his hands. Walking like a crazy man, walking and afraid, half-awake. He didn't remember unlocking the cellar door, getting the scythe, but here he was in the moonlight, walking in the grain.

Among these grains there were many who were old, weary, wanting so very much to sleep. The long, quiet, moonless sleep.

The scythe held him, grew into his palms, forced him to walk.

Somehow, struggling, he got free of it. He threw it down, ran off into the wheat, where he stopped and went down on his knees.

"I don't want to kill anymore," he said. "If I work with the scythe I'll have to kill Molly and the kids. Don't ask me to do that!"

The stars only sat in the sky, shining.

Behind him, he heard a dull, thumping sound.

Something shot up over the hill into the sky. It was like a living thing, with arms of red colour, licking at the stars. Sparks fell into his face. The thick, hot odour of fire came with it.

The house!

Crying out, he got sluggishly, hopelessly, to his feet, looking at the big fire.

The little white house with the live oaks was roaring up in one savage bloom of fire. Heat rolled over the hill and he swam in it and went down in it, stumbling, drowning over his head.

By the time he got down the hill there was not a shingle, bolt or threshold of it that wasn't alive with flame. It made blistering, crackling, fumbling noises.

No one screamed inside. No one ran around or shouted.

He yelled in the yard. "Molly! Susie! Drew!"

He got no answer. He ran close in until his eyebrows withered and his skin crawled hot like paper burning, crisping, curling up in tight little curls.

# THE SCYTHE

"Molly! Susie!"

The fire settled contentedly down to feed. Drew ran around the house a dozen times, all alone, trying to find a way in. Then he sat where the fire roasted his body and waited until the last ceilings bent, blanketing the floors with molten plaster and scorched lathing. Until the flames died and smoke coughed up, and the new day came slowly; and there was nothing but embering ashes and an acid smouldering.

Disregarding the heat fanning from the levelled frames Drew walked into the ruin. It was still too dark to see much. Red light glowed on his sweating throat. He stood like a stranger in a new and different land. Here – the kitchen. Charred tables, chairs, the iron stove, the cupboards. Here – the hall. Here the parlour and then over here was the bedroom where –

Where Molly was still alive.

She slept among the fallen timbers and angry-coloured pieces of wire spring and metal.

She slept as if nothing had happened. Her small white hands lay at her sides, flaked with sparks. Her calm face slept with a flaming lath across one cheek.

Drew stopped and didn't believe it. In the ruin of her smoking bedroom she lay on a glittering bed of sparks, her skin intact, her breast rising, falling, taking air.

"Molly!"

Alive and sleeping after the fire, after the walls had roared down, after ceilings had collapsed upon her and flame had lived all about her.

His shoes smoked as he pushed through piles of fuming litter. It could have seared his feet off at the ankles, he wouldn't have known.

"Molly . . ."

He bent over her. She didn't move or hear him, and she didn't speak. She wasn't dead. She wasn't alive. She just lay there with the fire surrounding her and not touching her, not harming her in any way. Her cotton nightgown was streaked with ashes, but not burnt. Her brown hair was pillowed on a tumble of red-hot coals.

He touched her cheek, and it was cold, cold in the middle of hell. Tiny breaths trembled her half-smiling lips.

The children were there, too. Behind a veil of smoke he made out two smaller figures huddled in the ashes sleeping. He carried all three of them out to the edge of the wheat field.

"Molly. Molly, wake up! Kids! Kids, wake up!"

They breathed and didn't move and went on sleeping.

"Kids, wake up! Your mother is −"

Dead? No, not dead. But −

He shook the kids as if they were to blame. They paid no attention; they were busy with their dreams. He put them back down and stood over them, his face cut with lines.

He knew why they'd slept through the fire and continued to sleep now. He knew why Molly just lay there, never wanting to laugh again.

The power of the wheat and scythe.

Their lives, supposed to end yesterday, May 30th, 1938, had

been prolonged simply because he refused to cut the grain. They should have died in the fire. That's the way it was meant to *be*. But since he had not used the scythe, nothing could hurt them. A house had flamed and fallen and still they lived, caught halfway, not dead, not alive. Simply – waiting. And all over the world thousands more just like them, victims of accidents, fires, disease, suicide, waited, slept just like Molly and her children slept. Not able to die, not able to live. All because a man was afraid of harvesting the ripe grain. All because one man thought he could stop working with a scythe and never work with that scythe again.

He looked down upon the children. The job had to be done every day and every day with never a stopping but going on, with never a pause, but always the harvesting, forever and forever and forever.

*All right*, he thought. *All right. I'll use the scythe.*

He didn't say goodbye to his family. He turned with a slow-feeding anger and found the scythe and walked rapidly, then he began to trot, then he ran with long jolting strides into the field, raving, feeling the hunger in his arms, as the wheat whipped and flailed his legs. He pounded through it, shouting. He stopped.

"Molly!" he cried, and raised the blade and swung it down.

"Susie!" he cried. "Drew!" And swung the blade down again.

Somebody screamed. He didn't turn to look at the fire-ruined house.

And then, sobbing wildly, he rose above the grain again and

again and hewed to left and right and to left and to right. Over and over and over! Slicing out huge scars in green wheat and ripe wheat, with no selection and no care, cursing, over and over, swearing, laughing, the blade swinging up in the sun and falling in the sun with a singing whistle! Down!

Bombs shattered London, Moscow, Tokyo.

The blade swung insanely.

And the kilns of Belsen and Buchenwald took fire.

The blade sang, crimson wet.

And mushrooms vomited out blind suns at White Sands, Hiroshima, Bikini, and up through, and in continental Siberian skies.

The grain wept in a green rain, falling.

Korea, Indo-China, Egypt, India trembled; Asia stirred, Africa woke in the night . . .

And the blade went on rising, crashing, severing, with the fury and the rage of a man who has lost and lost so much that he no longer cares what he does to the world.

Just a few short miles off the main highway, down a rough dirt road that leads to nowhere, just a few short miles from a highway jammed with traffic bound for California.

Once in a while during the long years a jalopy gets off the main highway, pulls up steaming in front of the charred ruin of a little white house at the end of the dirt road, to ask instructions from the farmer they see just beyond, the one who works insanely, wildly, without ever stopping, night and day, in the endless fields of wheat.

But they get no help and no answer. The farmer in the field

is too busy, even after all these years; too busy slashing and chopping the green wheat instead of the ripe.

And Drew Erickson moves on with his scythe, with the light of blind suns and a look of white fire in his never-sleeping eyes, on and on and on . . .

# A SEA ABOVE THE SKY

## THOMAS WRIGHT, 1844

*from* Ten Thousand Wonderful Things,
*edited by Edmund Fillingham King*

*This is an excerpt from a Victorian book called* Ten Thousand
Wonderful Things: "*comprising whatever is marvellous and
rare, curious, eccentric, and extraordinary, in all ages and
nations." I paid five pounds for it years ago at an antiques fair
and my family said it was a waste of money. It wasn't, though.
I wrote a story called "The Sky Sea", and the poet Seamus
Heaney has written of a similar incident. Truth is stranger than
fiction . . .?*

THIS BELIEF IS curiously illustrated by two legendary
stories preserved by Gervase of Tilbury.

"One Sunday," he says, "the people of a village in England
were coming out of church on a thick cloudy day, when they
saw the anchor of a ship hooked to one of the tombstones; the
cable, which was tightly stretched, hanging down from the air.
The people were astonished, and while they were consulting
about it, suddenly they saw the rope move as though someone
laboured to pull up the anchor. The anchor, however, still held
fast by the stone, and a great noise was suddenly heard in the
air, like the shouting of sailors. Presently a sailor was seen

sliding down the cable for the purpose of unfixing the anchor; and when he had just loosened it, the villagers seized hold of him, and while in their hands he quickly died, just as though he had been drowned. About an hour after, the sailors above, hearing no more of their comrade, cut the cable and sailed away.

"In memory of this extraordinary event, the people of the village made the hinges of the church doors out of the iron of the anchor, and there they are still to be seen.

"At another time, a merchant of Bristol set sail with his cargo for Ireland. Some time after this, while his family were at supper, a knife suddenly fell in through the window on the table. When the husband returned, he saw the knife, declared it to be his own, and said that on such a day, at such an hour, while sailing in an unknown part of the sea, he dropped the knife overboard, and the day and hour were known to be exactly the time when it fell through the window." These accidents, Gervase thinks, "are a clear proof of there being a sea above hanging over us."

# A VINE ON A HOUSE

## AMBROSE BIERCE

ABOUT THREE MILES from the little town of Norton, in Missouri, on the road leading to Maysville, stands an old house that was last occupied by a family named Harding. Since 1886 no one has lived in it, nor is anyone likely to live in it again. Time and the disfavour of persons dwelling thereabout are converting it into a rather picturesque ruin. An observer unacquainted with its history would hardly put it into the category of "haunted houses", yet in all the region round such is its evil reputation. Its windows are without glass, its doorways without doors; there are wide breaches in the shingle roof, and for lack of paint the weatherboarding is a dun grey. But these unfailing signs of the supernatural are partly concealed and greatly softened by the abundant foliage of a large vine overrunning the entire structure. This vine – of a species which no botanist has ever been able to name – has an important part in the story of the house.

The Harding family consisted of Robert Harding, his wife Matilda, Miss Julia Went, who was her sister, and two young children. Robert Harding was a silent, cold-mannered man who made no friends in the neighbourhood and apparently cared to make none. He was about forty years old, frugal and industrious, and made a living from the little farm which is now overgrown with brush and brambles. He and his sister-in-law were rather tabooed by their neighbours, who seemed to think that they were seen too frequently together – not entirely their fault, for at these times they evidently did not challenge observation. The moral code of rural Missouri is stern and exacting.

Mrs Harding was a gentle, sad-eyed woman, lacking a left foot.

At some time in 1884 it became known that she had gone to visit her mother in Iowa. That was what her husband said in reply to inquiries, and his manner of saying it did not encourage further questioning. She never came back, and two years later, without selling his farm or anything that was his, or appointing an agent to look after his interests, or removing his household goods, Harding, with the rest of the family, left the country. Nobody knew whither he went; nobody at that time cared. Naturally, whatever was movable about the place soon disappeared and the deserted house became "haunted" in the manner of its kind.

One summer evening, four or five years later, the Revd J. Gruber, of Norton, and a Maysville attorney named Hyatt met on horseback in front of the Harding place. Having business matters to discuss, they hitched their animals and, going to the house, sat on the porch to talk. Some humorous reference to the sombre reputation of the place was made and forgotten as soon as uttered, and they talked of their business affairs until it grew almost dark. The evening was oppressively warm, the air stagnant.

Presently both men started from their seats in surprise: a long vine that covered half the front of the house and dangled its branches from the edge of the porch above them was visibly and audibly agitated, shaking violently in every stem and leaf.

"We shall have a storm," Hyatt exclaimed.

Gruber said nothing, but silently directed the other's attention to the foliage of adjacent trees, which showed no movement; even the delicate tips of the boughs silhouetted against the clear sky were motionless. They hastily passed down the steps to what had been a lawn and looked upward at the vine, whose entire length was now visible. It continued in violent agitation, yet they could discern no disturbing cause.

"Let us leave," said the minister.

And leave they did. Forgetting that they had been travelling in opposite directions, they rode away together. They went to Norton, where they related their strange experience to several discreet friends. The next evening, at about the same hour, accompanied by two others whose names are not recalled, they were again on the porch of the Harding house, and again the mysterious phenomenon occurred: the vine was violently agitated while under the closest scrutiny from root to tip, nor did their combined strength applied to the trunk serve to still it. After an hour's observation they retreated, no less wise, it is thought, than when they had come.

No great time was required for these singular facts to rouse the curiosity of the entire neighbourhood. By day and by night crowds of persons assembled at the Harding house "seeking a sign". It does not appear that any found it, yet so credible were the witnesses mentioned that none doubted the reality of the "manifestations" to which they testified.

By either a happy inspiration or some destructive design, it was one day proposed – nobody appeared to know from whom the suggestion came – to dig up the vine, and after a good deal of debate this was done. Nothing was found but the root, yet nothing could have been more strange!

For five or six feet from the trunk, which had at the surface of the ground a diameter of several inches, it ran downward, single and straight, into a loose, friable earth; then it divided and subdivided into rootlets, fibres and filaments, most curiously interwoven. When carefully freed from soil they showed a singular formation. In their ramifications and doublings back upon themselves they made a compact network, having in size and shape an amazing resemblance to the human figure. Head, trunk and limbs were there; even the fingers and toes were distinctly defined; and many professed to see in the distribution and arrangement of the fibres in the globular mass representing the head a grotesque suggestion of a face. The figure was horizontal; the smaller roots had begun to unite at the breast.

In point of resemblance to the human form this image was imperfect. At about ten inches from one of the knees, the cilia forming that leg had abruptly doubled backward and inward upon their course of growth. The figure lacked the left foot.

There was but one inference – the obvious one; but in the ensuing excitement as many courses of action were proposed as there were incapable counsellors. The matter was settled by the sheriff of the county, who as the lawful custodian of the abandoned estate ordered the root replaced and the excavation filled with the earth that had been removed.

Later inquiry brought out only one fact of relevancy and significance: Mrs Harding had never visited her relatives in Iowa, nor did they know that she was supposed to have done so.

Of Robert Harding and the rest of his family nothing is known. The house retains its evil reputation, but the replanted vine is as orderly and well-behaved a vegetable as a nervous person could wish to sit under of a pleasant night, when the katydids grate out their immemorial revelation and the distant whippoorwill signifies his notion of what ought to be done about it.

# THE MASTER

## DIANA WYNNE JONES

THIS IS THE trouble with being a newly qualified vet. The call came at 5.50 a.m. I thought it was a man's voice, though it was high for a man, and I didn't quite catch the name – Harry Sanovit? Harrison Ovett? Anyway, he said it was urgent.

Accordingly, I found myself on the edge of a plain, facing a dark fir forest. It was about mid-morning. The fir trees stood dark and evenly spaced, exhaling their crackling gummy scent, with vistas of trodden-looking pine-needles beneath them. *A wolfwood*, I thought. I was sure that thought was right. The spacing of the trees was so regular that it suggested an artificial pinewood in the zoo, and there was a kind of humming, far down at the edges of the senses, as if machinery was at work sustaining a manmade environment here. The division between trees and plain was so sharp that I had some doubts that I would be able to enter the wood.

But I stepped inside with no difficulty. Under the trees it was cooler, more strongly scented, and full of an odd kind of depression which made me sure that there was some sort of danger here. I walked on the carpet of needles cautiously, relaxed but intensely afraid. There seemed to be some kind of path winding between the straight boles and I followed it into the heart of the wood. After a few turns, flies buzzed round something just off the path. *Danger!* pricked out all over my skin like sweat, but I went and looked all the same.

It was a young woman about my own age. From the flies and the freshness, I would have said she had been killed only hours ago. Her throat had been torn out. The expression on her half-averted face was of sheer terror. She had glorious red hair and was wearing what looked, improbably, to be evening dress.

I backed away, swallowing. As I backed, something came up beside me. I whirled round with a croak of terror.

"No need to fear," he said. "I am only the fool."

He was very tall and thin and ungainly. His feet were in big laced boots, jigging a silent ingratiating dance on the pine-needles, and the rest of his clothes were dull brown and close fitting. His huge hands came out to me placatingly. "I am Egbert," he said. "You may call me Eggs. You will take no harm if you stay with me." His eyes slid off mine apologetically, round and blue-grey. He grinned all over his small inane face. Under his close crop of straw-fair hair, his face was indeed that of a near-idiot. He did not seem to notice the woman's corpse at all, even though he seemed to know I was full of horror.

"What's going on here?" I asked him helplessly. "I'm a vet, not a – not a – mortician. What animal needs me?"

He smiled seraphically at nothing over my left shoulder. "I am only Eggs, Lady. I don't not know nothing. What you need to do is call the Master. Then you will know."

"So where is the Master?" I said.

He looked baffled by this question. "Hereabouts," he suggested. He gave another beguiling smile, over my right shoulder this time, panting slightly. "He will come if you call him right. Will I show you the house, Lady? There are rare sights there."

"Yes, if you like," I said. Anything to get away from whatever had killed that girl. Besides, I trusted him somehow. The way he had said I would take no harm if I was with him had been said in a way I believed.

He turned and cavorted up the path ahead of me, skipping soundlessly on his great feet, waving great gangling arms, clumsily tripping over a tree root and, even more clumsily, just saving himself. He held his head on one side and hummed as he went, happy and harmless. That is to say, harmless to me so far. Though he walked like a great hopping puppet, those huge hands were certainly strong enough to rip a throat out.

"Who killed that girl?" I asked him. "Was it the Master?"

His head snapped round, swayingly, and he stared at me, appalled, balancing the path as though it were a tightrope. "Oh no, Lady. The Master wouldn't not do that!" He turned sadly, almost tearfully away.

"I'm sorry," I said.

His head bent, acknowledging that he had heard, but he continued to walk the tightrope of the path without answering, and I followed. As I did, I was aware that there was something moving among the trees to either side of us. Something softly kept pace with us there and, I was sure, something also followed along the path behind. I did not try to see what it was. I was quite as much angry with myself as I was scared. I had let my shock at seeing that corpse get the better of my judgement. I saw I must wait to find out how the redheaded girl had got herself killed. *Caution!* I said to myself. *Caution!* This path was a tightrope indeed.

"Has the Master got a name?" I asked.

That puzzled Eggs. He stood balancing on the path to think. After a moment he nodded doubtfully, shot me a shy smile over his shoulder and walked on. No attempt to ask my name, I noticed. As if I was the only other person there and "Lady" should be enough. Which meant that the presences among the trees and behind on the path were possibly not human.

Round the next bend, I found myself facing the verandah of a chalet-like building. It looked a little as if it were made of wood, but it was no substance that I knew. Eggs tripped on the step and floundered towards the door at the back of the verandah. Before I could make more than a move to help him he had saved himself and his great hands were groping with an incomprehensible lock on the door. The humming was more evident here. I had been hoping that what I had heard at the edge of the wood had been the flies on the corpse. It was not. Though the sound was still not much more than a vibration at the edge of the mind, I knew I had been right in my first idea. Something artificial was being maintained here, and whatever was maintaining it seemed to be under this house.

*In this house*, I thought, as Eggs got the door open and

floundered inside ahead of me. The room we entered was full of – well, devices. The nearest thing was a great cauldron, softly bubbling for no reason I could see, and giving out a gauzy violet light. The other things were arranged in ranks beyond, bewilderingly. In one place something grotesque stormed green inside a design painted on the floor; here a copper bowl smoked; there a single candle sat like something holy on a white stone; a knife suspended in air dripped gently into a jar of rainbow glass. Much of it was glass, twinkling, gleaming, chiming, under the light from the low ceiling that seemed to come from nowhere. There were no windows.

"Good heavens!" I said, disguising my dismay as amazement. "What are all these?"

Eggs grinned. "I know some. Pretty, aren't they?" He roved surging about, touching the edge of a pattern here, passing his huge hand through a flame or a column of smoke there, causing a shower of fleeting white stars, solemn gong-notes and a rich smell of incense. "Pretty, aren't they?" he kept repeating, and, "*Very* pretty!" as an entire fluted glass structure began to ripple and change shape at the end of the room. As it changed, the humming which was everywhere in the room changed too. It became a purring chime and I felt an indescribable pulling-feeling from the roots of my hair and under my skin, almost as if the glass thing was trying to change me as it changed itself.

"I should come away from that if I were you," I said as firmly and calmly as I could manage.

Eggs turned and came floundering towards me, grinning

eagerly. To my relief, the sound from the glass modulated to a new kind of humming. But my relief vanished when Eggs said, "Petra knew all, before Annie tore her throat out. Do you know as much as Petra? You are clever, Lady, as well as beautiful." His eyes slid across me, respectfully. Then he turned and hung, lurching, over the cauldron with the gauzy violet light. "Petra took pretty dresses from here," he said. "Would you like for me to get you a pretty dress?"

"Not at the moment, thank you," I said, trying to sound kind. As I said, Eggs was not necessarily harmless. "Show me the rest of the house," I said, to distract him.

He fell over his feet to oblige. "Come. See here." He led me to the side of the devices, where there was a clear passage and some doors. At the back of the room was another door which slid open by itself as we came near. Eggs giggled proudly at that, as if it was his doing. Beyond was evidently a living-room. The floor here was soft, carpet-like and blue. Darker blue blocks hung about, mysteriously half a metre or so in the air. Four of them were a metre or so square. The fifth was two metres each way. They had the look of a suite of chairs and a sofa to me. A squiggly mural-thing occupied one wall and the entire end wall was window, which seemed to lead to another verandah, beyond which I could see a garden of some kind. "The room is pretty, isn't it?" Eggs asked anxiously. "I like the room."

I assured him I liked the room. This relieved him. He stumbled around a floating blue block, which was barely disturbed by his falling against it, and pressed a plate in the wall beyond. The long glass of the window slid back, leaving the room open to the verandah. He turned to me, beaming.

"Clever," I said, and made another cautious attempt to find out more. "Did Petra show you how to open that, or was it the Master?"

He was puzzled again. "I don't not know," he said, worried about it.

I gave up and suggested we went into the garden. He was pleased. We went over the verandah and down steps into a rose garden. It was an oblong shape, carved out from among the fir-trees, about fifteen metres from the house to the bushy hedge at the far end. And it was as strange as everything else. The square of sky overhead was subtly the wrong colour, as if you were seeing it through sunglasses. It made the colour of the roses rich and too dark. I walked through it with a certainty that it was being maintained – or created – by one of the devices in that windowless room.

The roses were all standards, each planted in a little circular bed. The head of each was about level with my head. No petals fell on the gravel-seeming paths. I kept exclaiming, because these were the most perfect roses I ever saw, whether full bloom, bud or overblown. When I saw an orange rose – the colour I love most – I put my hand up cautiously to make sure that it was real. It was. While my fingers lingered on it I happened to glance at Eggs towering over me. It was just a flick of the eyes, which I don't think he saw. He was standing there, smiling as always, staring at me intently. There was, I swear, another shape to his face and it was not the shape of an idiot. But it was not the shape of a normal man either. It was an intent, *hunting* face.

Next moment he was surging inanely forward. "I will pick you a rose, Lady." He reached out and stumbled as he reached. His hand caught a thorn in a tumble of petals. He snatched it back with a yelp. "Oh!" he said. "It hurts!" He lifted his hand and stared at it. Blood was running down the length of his little finger.

"Suck it," I said. "Is the thorn still in it?"

"I don't know," Eggs said helplessly. Several drops of blood had fallen among the fallen petals before he took my advice and sucked the cut, noisily. As he did so, his other hand came forward to bar my way. "Stay by me, Lady," he said warningly.

I had already stopped dead. Whether they had been there all along or had been summoned, materialized, by the scent of blood, I still do not know, but they were there now, against the hedge at the end of the garden, all staring at me. Three Alsatian dogs, I told myself foolishly and knew it was nonsense as I thought it. Three of them. Three wolves. Each of them must have been, in bulk if not in height, as least as big as I was.

They were dark in the curious darkness of that garden. Their eyes were the easiest to see, light wolf-green. All of them staring at me, staring earnestly, hungrily. The smaller two were crouched in front. One of those was brindled and larger and rangier than his browner companion. And these two were only small by comparison with the great black she-wolf standing behind with slaver running from her open jaws. She was poised either to pounce or to run away. I have never seen anything more feral than that black she-wolf. But they were all feral, stiff-legged, terrified, half in mind to tear my throat out, and yet they were held there for some reason, simply staring. All three were soundlessly snarling, even before I spoke.

My horror – caught from the wolves to some extent – was beyond thought and out into a dreamlike state, where I simply knew that Eggs was right when he said I would be safe with him, and so I said what the dream seemed to require. "Eggs," I said, "tell me their names."

Eggs was quite unperturbed. His hand left his mouth and pointed at the brindled wolf in front. "That one is Hugh, Lady. Theo is the one beside him. She standing at the back is Annie."

So now I knew what had torn red-headed Petra's throat out. *And what kind of a woman was she,* I wondered, *who must have had Eggs as servant and a roomful of strange devices, and on top of this gave three wild beasts these silly names?* My main thought was that I did not want my throat torn out too. And I had been called here as a vet after all. It took quite an effort to look those three creatures over professionally, but I did so. Ribs showed under the curly brownish coat of Theo. Hugh's haunches stuck out like knives. As for Annie standing behind, her belly clung upwards almost to her backbone. "When did they last eat?" I said.

Eggs smiled at me. "There is food in the forest for them, Lady."

I stared at him, but he seemed to have no idea what he was saying. It was to the wolves' credit that they did not seem to regard dead Petra as food, but from the look of them it would not be long before they did so. "Eggs," I said, "these three are starving. You and I must go back into the house and find food for them."

Eggs seemed much struck by this idea. "Clever," he said. "I am only the fool, Lady." And as I turned, gently, not to alarm the wolves, he stretched out his hands placatingly – at least, it looked placating, but it was quite near to an attempt to take hold of me, a sketch of it, as it were. That alarmed me, but I dared not show it here. The wolves' ears pricked a little as we moved off up the garden, but they did not move, to my great relief.

Back through the house Eggs led me in his lurching, puppet's gait, round the edges of the room with the devices, where the humming filled the air and still seemed to drag at me in a way I did not care for at all, to another brightly lit windowless room on the other side. It was a kitchen-place, furnished in what seemed to be glass. Here Eggs cannoned into a glass table and brought up, looking at me expectantly. I gazed round at glass-fronted apparatus, some of it full of crockery, some of it clearly food-stores, with food heaped behind the glass, and some of it quite mysterious to me. I made for the glass cupboard full of various joints of meat. I could see they were fresh, although the thing was clearly not a refrigerator. "How do you open this?" I asked.

Eggs looked down at his great hands, planted in encircling vapour on top of the glass table. "I don't not know, Lady."

I could have shaken him. Instead I clawed at the edges of

the cupboard. Nothing happened. There it was, warmish, piled with a good fifty kilograms of meat, while three starving wolves prowled outside, and nothing I could do seemed to have any effect on the smooth edge of the glass front. At length I pried my fingernails under the top edge and pulled, thinking it moved slightly.

Eggs' huge hand knocked against mine, nudging me awkwardly away. "No, no, Lady. That way you'll get hurt. It is under stass-spell, see." For a moment he fumbled doubtfully at the top rim of the glass door, but, when I made a movement to come back and help, his hands suddenly moved, smoothly and surely. The thing clicked. The glass slid open downwards and the smell of meat rolled out into the kitchen.

*So you do know how to do it!* I thought. *And I* knew *you did!* There was some hint he had given me, I knew, as I reached for the nearest joint, which I could not quite see now.

"No, no, Lady!" This time Eggs pushed me aside hard. He was really distressed. "Never put hand into stass-spell. It will die on you. You do this." He took up a long shiny pair of tongs which I had not noticed because they were nested into the top of the cupboard, and grasped the nearest joint with them. "This, Lady?"

"And two more," I said. "And when did you last eat, Eggs?" He shrugged and looked at me, baffled. "Then get out those two steaks too," I said. Eggs seemed quite puzzled, but he fetched out the meat. "Now we must find water for them as well," I said.

"But there is juice here in this corner!" Eggs objected.

"See." He went to one of the mysterious fixtures and shortly came back with a sort of cardboard cup swaying in one hand, which he handed me to taste, staring eagerly while I did. "Good?" he asked.

It was some form of alcohol. "Very good," I said, "but not for wolves." It took me half an hour of patient work to persuade Eggs to fetch out a large lightweight bowl and then to manipulate a queer faucet to fill it with water. He could not see the point of it at all. I was precious near to hitting him before long. I was quite glad when he stayed behind in the kitchen to shut the cabinets and finish his cup of "juice".

The wolves had advanced down the garden. I could see their pricked ears and their eyes above the verandah boards, but they did not move when I stepped out on to the verandah. I had to make myself move with a calmness and slowness I was far from feeling. Deliberately, I dropped each joint, one by one, with a sticky thump on to the strange surface. From the size and the coarse grain of the meat, it seemed to be venison – at least, I hoped it was. Then I carefully lowered the bowl to stand at the far end of the verandah, looking all the time through my hair at the wolves. They did not move, but the open jaws of the big wolf, Annie, were dripping.

The bowl down, I backed away into the living-room, where I just had to sit down on the nearest blue block. My knees gave.

They did not move for long seconds. Then all three disappeared below the verandah and I thought they must have slunk away. But the two smaller ones reappeared, suddenly, silently, as if they had materialized, at the end of the verandah beside the bowl. Tails trailing, shaking all over, they crept towards it. Both stuck their muzzles in and drank avidly. I could hear their frantic lapping. And when they raised their heads, which they both did shortly, neatly and disdainfully, I realized that one of the joints of meat had gone. The great wolf, Annie, had been and gone.

Her speed must have reassured Theo and Hugh. Both sniffed the air, then turned and trotted towards the remaining joints. Each nosed a joint. Each picked it up neatly in his jaws. Theo seemed about to jump down into the garden with his. But Hugh, to my astonishment, came straight towards the open window, evidently intending to eat on the carpet as dogs do.

He never got a chance. Theo dropped his joint and sprang at him with a snarl. There was the heavy squeak of clawed paws. Hugh sprang round, hackles rising the length of his lean sloping back, and snarled back without dropping his portion. It was, he seemed to be saying, his own business where he went to eat. Theo, crouching, advancing on him with lowered head and white teeth showing, was clearly denying him this right. I braced myself for the fight. But at that moment, Annie reappeared, silent as ever, head and great forepaws on the edge of the verandah, and stood there, poised. Theo and Hugh vanished like smoke, running long and low to either side. Both took their food with them, to my relief. Annie dropped out of sight again. Presently there were faint, very faint, sounds of eating from below.

I went back to the glassy kitchen, where I spent the next few hours getting Eggs to eat too. He did not seem to regard anything in the kitchen as edible. It took me a good hour to persuade him to open a vegetable cabinet and quite as long to persuade him to show me how to cook the food. If I became insistent, he said, "I don't not know, Lady," lost interest and shuffled off to the windowless room to play with the pretty lights. That alarmed me. Every time I fetched him back, the humming chime from the glass apparatus seemed to drag at me more intensely. I tried pleading. "Eggs, I'm going to cut these yams, but I can't find a knife somehow." That worked better. Eggs would come over obliging and find me a thing like a prong and then wander off to his "juice" again. There were times when I thought we were going to have to eat everything raw.

But it got done in the end. Eggs showed me how to ignite a terrifying heat-source that was totally invisible and I fried the food on it in a glass skillet. Most of the vegetables were quite strange to me, but at least the steak was recognizable. We were just sitting down on glass stools to eat it at the glass table, when a door I had not realized was there slid aside beside me. The garden was beyond. The long snout of Hugh poked through the gap. The pale eyes met mine and the wet nose quivered wistfully.

"What do you want?" I said and I knew I had jerked with fear. It was obvious what Hugh wanted. The garden must have filled with the smell of cooking. But I had not realized that the wolves could get into the kitchen when they pleased. Trying to seem calm, I tossed Hugh some fat I'd trimmed off the steaks. He caught it neatly and, to my intense relief, backed out of the door, which closed behind him.

I was almost too shaken to eat after that, but Eggs ate his share with obvious pleasure, though he kept glancing at me as if he was afraid I would think he was making a pig of himself. It was both touching and irritating. But the food – and the "juice" – did him good. His face became pinker and he did not jig so much. I began to risk a few cautious questions. "Eggs, did Petra live in this house or just work here?"

He looked baffled. "I don't know."

"But she used the wolves to help her in her work, didn't she?" It seemed clear to me that they *must* have been laboratory animals in some way.

Eggs shifted on his stool. "I don't not know," he said unhappily.

"And did the Master help in the work too?" I persisted.

But this was too much for Eggs. He sprang up in agitation and, before I could stop him, he swept everything off the table into a large receptacle near the door. "I can't say!" I heard him say above the crash of breaking crockery.

After that he would listen to nothing I said. His one idea was that we must go to the living-room. "To sit elegantly, Lady," he explained. "And I will bring the sweet foods and the juice to enjoy ourselves with there."

There seemed no stopping him. He surged out of the kitchen with an armload of peculiar receptacles and a round jug of "juice" balanced between those and his chin, weaving this way and that among the devices in the windowless room. These flared and flickered and the unsupported knife danced in the air as I pursued him. I felt as much as saw the fluted glass structure changing shape again. The sound of it dragged at the very roots of me.

"Eggs," I said desperately. "How do I call the Master? Please."

"I can't say," he said, reeling on into the living-room.

Some enlightenment came to me. Eggs meant exactly what he said. I had noticed that when he said "I don't *not* know," this did not mean that he did not know: it usually seemed to be something he could not explain. Now I saw that when he said, "I can't say", he meant that he was, for some reason, unable to tell me about the Master. *So*, I thought, struggling on against the drag of the chiming apparatus, *this means I must use a little cunning to get him to tell me.*

In the living-room Eggs was laying out dishes of sweets and little balls of cheese near the centre of the large blue sofa-like block. I sat down at one end of it. Eggs promptly came and sat beside me, grinning and breathing "juice" fumes. I got up and moved to the other end of the sofa. Eggs took the hint. He stayed where he was, sighing, and poured himself another papery cup of his "juice."

"Eggs," I began. Then I noticed that the wolf, Hugh, was couched on the verandah facing into the room, with his brindled nose on his paws and his sharp haunches outlined against the sunset roses. Beyond him were the backs of the two others, apparently asleep. Well, wolves always leave one at least of their pack on guard when they sleep. I told myself that Hugh had drawn sentry duty and went back to thinking how I could induce Eggs to tell me how to get hold of this Master. By this time I felt I would go mad unless someone explained this situation to me.

"Eggs," I began again, "when I ask you how I fetch the Master, you tell me you can't say, isn't that right?" He nodded eagerly, obligingly, and offered me a sweet. I took it. I was doing well so far. "That means that something's stopping you telling me, doesn't it?" That lost him. His eyes slid from mine. I looked where his eyes went and found that Hugh had been moving, in the unnoticed silent way a wild creature can. He was now crouched right inside the room. The light feral eyes were fixed on me. *Help!* I thought. But I had to go on with what I was saying before Eggs' crazed mind lost it. "So I'm going to take it that when you say, 'I can't say', you mean 'Yes', Eggs. It's going to be like a game."

Eggs' face lit up. "I like games, Lady!"

"Good," I said. "The game is called Calling the Master. Now I know you can't tell me direct how to call him, but the rule is that you're allowed to give me hints."

That was a mistake. "And what is the hint, Lady?" Eggs asked, in the greatest delight. "Tell me and I will give it."

"Oh – I – er —" I said. And I felt something cold gently touch my hand. I looked down to find Hugh standing by my knees. Beyond him, Theo was standing up, bristling. "What do you want now?" I said to Hugh. His eyes slid across the plates of sweets and he sighed, like a dog. "Not sweets," I said firmly.

Hugh understood. He laid his long head on my knee, yearningly.

This produced a snarl from Theo out on the verandah. It sounded like pure jealousy.

"You can come in too, if you want, Theo," I said hastily. Theo gave no sign of understanding, but when I next looked he was half across the threshold. He was crouched, not lying. His hackles were up and his eyes glared at Hugh. Hugh's eyes moved to see where he was, but he did not raise his chin from my knee.

All this so unnerved me that I tried to explain what a hint was by telling Eggs a story. I should have known better. "In this story," I said, absently stroking Hugh's head as if he were my dog. Theo instantly rose to his feet with the lips of his muzzle back and his ears up. I removed my hand – but quick! "In this story," I said. Theo lay down again, but now it was me he was glaring at. "A lady was left three boxes by her father, one box gold, one silver and one lead. In one of the boxes there was a picture of her. Her father's orders were that the man who guessed which of the three boxes her picture was in could marry her –"

Eggs bounced up with a triumphant laugh. "I know! It was in the lead box! Lead protects. I can marry her!" He rolled about in delight. "Are you that lady?" he asked eagerly.

I suppressed a strong need to run about screaming. I was sure that if I did, either Theo or Annie would go for me. I was not sure about Hugh. He seemed to have been a house-pet. "Right," I said. "It was in the lead box, Eggs. This *other* lady knew that, but the men who wanted to marry her had to guess. All of them guessed wrong, until one day a beautiful man came along, whom this *other* lady wanted to marry. So what did she do?"

"Told him," said Eggs.

"No, she was forbidden to do that," I said. *God give me patience!* "Just like you. She had to give the man hints instead. Just like you. Before he came to choose the box, she got people to sing him a song and – remember it was the *lead* box – every line in that song rhymed with 'lead'. A rhyme is a word that sounds the same," I added hurriedly, seeing bewilderment cloud in Eggs' face. "You know – 'said' and 'bled' and 'red' all rhyme with 'lead'."

"Said, bled, red," Eggs repeated, quite lost.

"Dead, head," I said. Hugh's cold nose nudged my hand again. Wolves are not usually scavengers, unless in dire need, but I thought cheese would not hurt him. I passed him a round to keep him quiet.

Theo sprang up savagely and came half across the room. At the same instant, Eggs grasped what a rhyme was. "Fed, instead, bed, wed!" he shouted, rolling about with glee. I stared into Theo's grey-green glare and at his pleated lip showing the fangs beneath it, and prayed to heaven. Very slowly and carefully, I rolled a piece of cheese off the sofa towards him. Theo swung away from it and stalked back to the window. "My hint is bedspread, Lady!" Eggs shouted.

Hugh, meanwhile, calmly took his cheese as deftly and gently as any hunting-dog and sprang up on to the sofa beside me, where he stood with his head down, chewing with small bites to make the cheese last. "Now you've done it, Hugh!" I said, looking nervously at Theo's raked-up back and at the sharp outline of Annie beyond him.

"Thread, head, watershed, bread!" bawled Eggs. I realized he was drunk. His face was flushed and his eyes glittered. He had been putting back quantities of "juice" ever since he first showed me the kitchen. "Do I get to marry you now, Lady?" he asked soulfully.

Before I could think what to reply, Hugh moved across like lightning and bit Eggs on his nearest large folded knee. He jumped clear even quicker, as Eggs surged to his feet, and streaked off to join Theo on the verandah. I heard Theo snap at him.

Eggs took an uncertain step that way, then put his hand to his face. "What is this?" he said. "This room is chasing its tail." It was clear the "juice" had caught up with him.

"I think you're drunk," I said.

"Drink," said Eggs. "I must get a drink from the faucet. I am dying. It is worse than being remade." And he went blundering and crashing off into the windowless room.

I jumped up and went after him, sure that he would do untold damage bumping into cauldron or candle. But he wove his way through the medley of displays as only a drunk man can, avoiding each one by a miracle, and reached the kitchen when I was only half-way through the room. The hum of the crystal apparatus held me back. It dragged at my very skin. I had still only reached the cauldron when there was an appalling splintering crash from the kitchen, followed by a hoarse male scream.

I do not remember how I got to the kitchen. I only remember standing in the doorway, looking at Eggs kneeling in the remains of the glass table. He was clutching at his left arm with his right hand. Blood was pulsing steadily between his long fingers and making a pool on the glass-littered floor. The face he turned to me was so white that he looked as if he were wearing greasepaint. "What will you do, Lady?" he said.

*DO?* I thought. *I'm a vet. I can't be expected to deal with humans!* "For goodness sake, Eggs," I snapped at him. "Stop this messing about and get me the Master! Now. This instant!"

I think he said, "And I thought you'd never tell me!" But his voice was so far from human by then it was hard to be sure. His body boiled about on the floor, surging and seething and changing colour. In next to a second the thing on the floor was a huge grey wolf, with its back arched and its jaws wide in agony, pumping blood from a severed artery in its left foreleg.

At least I knew what to do with that. But before I could move, the door to the outside slid open to let in the great head and shoulders of Annie. I backed away. The look in those light, blazing eyes said, "You are not taking my mate like she did."

Here the chiming got into my head and proved to be the ringing of the telephone. My bedside clock said 5.55 a.m. I was quite glad to be rid of that dream as I fumbled the telephone up in the dark. "Yes?" I said, hoping I sounded as sleepy as I felt.

The voice was a light, high one, possibly a man's. "You won't know me," it said. "My name's Harrison Ovett and I'm in charge of an experimental project involving wild animals. We have a bit of an emergency on here. One of the wolves seems to be in quite a bad way. I'm sorry to call you out at such an hour, but —"

"It's my job," I said, too sleepy to be more than proud of the professional touch. "Where are you? How do I get to your project?"

I think he hesitated slightly. "It's a bit complicated to explain," he said. "Suppose I come and pick you up? I'll be outside in twenty minutes."

"Right," I said. And it was not until I put the phone down that I remembered my dream. The name was the same, I swear. I would equally swear to the voice. This is why I have spent the last twenty minutes feverishly dictating this account of my dream. If I get back safely, I'll erase it. But if I don't – well, I am not sure what anyone can do if Annie's torn my throat out, but at least someone will know what became of me. Besides, they say forewarned is forearmed. I have some idea what to expect.

# KING ARTHUR
## SIR THOMAS MALORY

*How King Arthur commanded to cast his sword Excalibur into the*
*water, and how he was delivered to ladies in a barge*

BUT I MAY not stand, mine head works so. Ah Sir Launcelot,
said King Arthur, this day have I sore missed thee: alas, that
ever I was against thee, for now have I my death, whereof Sir
Gawaine me warned in my dream. Then Sir Lucan took up
the king the one part, and Sir Bedivere the other part, and in
the lifting the king swooned; and Sir Lucan fell in a swoon
with the lift, that the part of his guts fell out of his body, and
therewith the noble knight's heart brast. And when the king
awoke, he beheld Sir Lucan, how he lay foaming at the mouth,
and part of his guts lay at his feet. Alas, said the king, this is to
me a full heavy sight, to see this noble duke so die for my sake,
for he would have holpen me, that had more need of help than
I. Alas, he would not complain him, his heart was so set to help
me: now Jesu have mercy upon his soul! Then Sir Bedivere
wept for the death of his brother. Leave this mourning and
weeping, said the king, for all this will not avail me, for wit
thou well an I might live myself, the death of Sir Lucan would

grieve me evermore; but my time hieth fast, said the king. Therefore, said Arthur unto Sir Bedivere, take thou Excalibur, my good sword, and go with it to yonder water side, and when thou comest there I charge thee throw my sword in that water, and come again and tell me what thou there seest. My lord, said Bedivere, your commandment shall be done, and lightly bring you word again. So Sir Bedivere departed, and by the way he beheld that noble sword, that the pommel and the haft was all of precious stones; and then he said to himself: If I throw this rich sword in the water, thereof shall never come good, but harm and loss. And then Sir Bedivere hid Excalibur under a tree. And so, as soon as he might, he came again unto the king, and said he had been at the water, and had thrown the sword in the water. What saw thou there? said the king. Sir, he said, I saw nothing but waves and winds. That is untruly said of thee, said the king, therefore go thou lightly again, and do my commandment; as thou art to me lief and dear, spare not, but throw it in. Then Sir Bedivere returned again, and took the sword in his hand; and then him thought sin and shame to throw away that noble sword, and so efte he hid the sword, and returned again, and told to the king that he had been at the water, and done his commandment. What saw thou there? said the king. Sir, he said, I saw nothing but the waters wappe and waves wanne. Ah, traitor untrue, said King Arthur, now hast thou betrayed me twice. Who would have weened that, thou that has been to me so lief and dear? and thou art named a noble knight, and would betray me for the richness of the sword. But now go again lightly, for thy long tarrying putteth me in great jeopardy of my life, for I have taken cold. And but if thou do now as I bid thee, if ever I may see thee, I shall slay thee with mine own hands; for thou wouldst for my rich sword see me dead. Then Sir Bedivere departed, and went to the sword, and lightly took it up, and went to the water side; and there he bound the girdle about the hilts, and then he threw the sword as far into the water, as he might; and there came an arm and an hand above the water and met it, and caught it, and so shook it thrice and brandished, and then vanished away the hand with the sword in the water. So Sir Bedivere came again to the king, and told him what he saw. Alas, said the king, help me hence, for I dread me I have tarried over long. Then Sir Bedivere took the king upon his back, and so went with him to that water side. And when they were at the water side, even fast by the bank hoved a little barge with many fair ladies in it, and among them all was a queen, and all they had black hoods, and all they wept and shrieked when they saw King Arthur. Now put me into the barge, said the king. And so he did softly; and there received him three queens with great mourning; and so they set them down, and in one of their laps King Arthur laid his head. And then that queen said: Ah, dear brother, why have ye tarried so long from me? alas, this wound on your head hath caught over-much cold. And so then they rowed from the land, and Sir Bedivere beheld all those ladies go from him. Then Sir Bedivere cried: Ah my lord Arthur, what shall become of me, now ye go from me and leave me here alone among mine enemies? Comfort thyself, said the king, and do as well as thou mayest, for in me is no trust for to trust in; for I will into the vale of Avilion to heal me of my grievous wound: and if thou hear never more of me, pray for my soul. But ever the queens and ladies wept and shrieked, that it was pity to hear. And as soon as Sir Bedivere had lost the sight of the barge, he wept and wailed, and so took the forest; and so he went all that night, and in the morning he was ware betwixt two holts hoar, of a chapel and an hermitage.

*How Sir Bedivere found him on the morrow dead in an hermitage, and how he abode there with the hermit*

Then was Sir Bedivere glad, and thither he went; and when he came into the chapel, he saw where lay an hermit grovelling on all four, there fast by a tomb was new graven. When the hermit saw Sir Bedivere he knew him well, for he was but little tofore Bishop of Canterbury, that Sir Mordred flemed. Sir, said Bedivere, what man is there interred that ye pray so fast for? Fair son, said the hermit, I wot not verily, but by deeming. But this night, at midnight, here came a number of ladies, and brought hither a dead corpse, and prayed me to bury him; and here they offered an hundred tapers, and they gave me an hundred besants. Alas, said Sir Bedivere, that was my lord King Arthur, that here lieth buried in this chapel. Then Sir Bedivere swooned; and when he awoke he prayed the hermit he might abide with him still there, to live with fasting and prayers. For from hence will I never go, said Sir Bedivere, by my will, but all the days of my life here to pray for my lord Arthur. Ye are welcome to me, said the hermit, for I know ye better than ye ween that I do. Ye are the bold Bedivere, and the full noble duke, Sir Lucan the Butler, was your brother. Then Sir Bedivere told the hermit all as ye have heard tofore. So there bode Sir Bedivere with the hermit that was tofore Bishop of Canterbury, and there Sir Bedivere put upon him poor clothes, and served the hermit full lowly in fasting and in prayers. Thus of Arthur I find never more written in books that be authorized, nor more of the very certainty of his death heard I never read, but thus was he led away in a ship wherein were three queens; that one was King Arthur's sister, Queen Morgan le Fay; the other was the Queen of Northgalis; the third was the Queen of the Waste Lands. Also there Nimue, the chief lady of the lake, that had wedded Pelleas the good knight; and this lady had done much for King Arthur, for she would never suffer Sir Pelleas to be in no place where he should be in danger of his life; and so he lived to the uttermost of his days with her in great rest. More of the death of King Arthur could I never find, but that ladies brought him to his burials; and such one was buried there, that the hermit bore witness that sometime was Bishop of Canterbury, but yet the hermit knew not in certain that he was verily the body of King Arthur: for this tale Sir Bedivere, knight of the Table Round, made it to be written.

# THE WHISPERER
## VIVIEN ALCOCK

THE TWO GIRLS walked silently down Appleford Road. They did not link arms or laugh or even look at one another. One of them looked miserable, almost frightened; the other was simply cross. No one would have taken them for best friends.

The cross one was the first to speak. She was a sturdy, freckled child, dressed with unaccustomed neatness in a cotton frock and white socks. Her hair was brushed and her fingernails clean.

"If it hurts that much to have me to tea, Charlotte," she said, "let's forget it."

"Don't be silly, Jane," the miserable one said, smiling with an effort. "If I hadn't wanted you to come, I wouldn't have invited you."

"You didn't," Jane pointed out. "I had to ask myself, remember?"

It still rankled. They had been best friends for several months now, and Jane had had Charlotte to tea hundreds of times. Never once had she been asked back. Her mother had begun to remark on it.

"Hullo, Charlotte, you here again?" she'd said; and then to Jane when they were alone, "Hasn't that child got a home of her own to go to?"

"She lives in Appleford Road," Jane had said, hoping to silence her mother, for Appleford Road was very grand.

"Then you'd think they could afford to have you to tea for a change," her mother had retorted.

Jane was a careless, generous child; it hadn't occurred to her before to wonder why Charlotte had never invited her home. But now a small doubt, like a piece of grit in a shoe, began to prick her mind. Was Charlotte secretly ashamed of her? Was she just making use of her till she found some grander, more suitable girl to go round with?

"No! Charlotte isn't like that!" she had told herself. "There must be some other reason." Deciding to put it to the test, she had invited herself to tea.

So here she was at last, walking beside her unwilling friend (if friend was the word for her) going angrily to tea where she wasn't wanted and no longer wished to go.

"This is it," Charlotte said suddenly. She had stopped in front of a green-painted garden door in a high wall. Looking up, Jane could see the roof and chimneys of a house beyond it, showing dark against the sky. A hidden house. A shut-away, secretive house, quite unlike its ostentatious neighbours.

*What have I got myself into?* she wondered, suddenly uneasy.

To her surprise, Charlotte did not open the garden door, but instead rang a bell set in the wall beside it, and stood waiting.

"D'you always keep it locked?" Jane asked.

"Yes."

"Why?"

Charlotte shrugged and did not answer.

The door opened. Jane did not know what she had expected, but it was certainly not what she saw. A garden bright with flowers, a crowd of people, all laughing and talking and holding out their hands: welcoming her with every appearance of joy.

"Here's Charlotte's little friend at last!"

"We've heard so much about you."

"Come in, come in, my dear."

"We've been longing to meet you."

She was hugged and kissed and introduced all round. To her surprise, there turned out to be only four of them; Charlotte's mother and father and two uncles. Somehow they had managed to fill the garden with so much noise and gaiety, that Jane kept looking round to see if there was anyone she had missed.

It was the same when they sat down to tea. Huge mirrors on every wall reflected the loaded table. Silver teapots glittered wherever she looked, plates of cakes, dishes of crimson and emerald jellies multiplied themselves in endless reflections, and the laughing, chattering family became a multitude.

*One, two, three, four of them*, Jane counted silently. *And Charlotte and me makes six. The others are just in the mirrors. Why do I keep feeling there's someone else here? Perhaps there's a dog under the table.*

She glanced down, but the long white tablecloth swept past

her knees to the floor. She had no time to puzzle further, before she was drawn into the conversation. Her opinion was sought on this and that. Smiling questions were showered on her from all sides, so quick and so many she hardly had time to answer before the next one came. They flattered her, teased her gently, laughed uproariously when she ventured a joke.

*I'm a success*, she thought. *They like me.*

Glowing with pleasure, she looked across at Charlotte; and found her friend too was chattering and smiling. Jane had never known her so talkative before. Charlotte's eyes were brilliant and there was a feverish flush on her cheeks.

Feverish? Why had that word come into her head? Why wouldn't it go away again?

Suddenly, in spite of the sparkling room, Jane felt a growing uneasiness. She looked round the table and it seemed to her now that the people were as unreal as their reflections in the mirrors. There was something unnatural about them. Why did they all talk so much? Laugh so loudly? It was as if they were weaving a fence of sound to keep something out.

Again, and more strongly, she sensed there was someone else there. Someone she had not seen. She looked round, but there were no dark corners, no cupboards or hiding places. There was only the table, and its concealing cloth . . .

She let her napkin slide off her knees, as if by accident, and bent down to pick it up, hoping to lift the edge of the cloth at the same time. But one of the uncles bent down as quickly and their heads collided with a dull thud. In the instant of silence that followed this, Jane heard an urgent whisper, soft and plaintive, a child's voice.

"Please, please let me in . . ." it said.

Then they were all talking again, as loudly as ever, drowning out the small voice. Asking her if she was all right, apologizing for the mishap, feeling her head for bumps, offering her more tea, and when she refused, suggesting she and Charlotte should go and play in the park . . .

"It's a lovely park, isn't it, Charlotte?"

"There's swings and seesaws."

"And ducks, don't forget the ducks!"

"And a grass bank to roll down. You'll love it there."

They had all got up together. Charlotte took her arm and pulled her towards the front door, while the others clustered behind her, still talking.

*They want to get me out of the house*, Jane thought, and, suddenly angry, she said loudly, "Can't I see your room first, Charlotte?"

Again, in the fleeting silence that followed her request, she heard the child's whisper.

"Let me in! Let . . ."

Then they were all talking again. Of course she must see Charlotte's room. They would all go and see Charlotte's room. They would have a party there and play noisy games. Wouldn't that be fun? Then they'd all go to the park.

As they trooped upstairs, Jane managed to get next to Charlotte. She whispered fiercely in her ear, "Who's that child?"

But Charlotte did not seem to hear her. She was smiling and talking. Talking, talking. They were all talking together as if they would never stop. The sound of their voices pounded in Jane's head, until she longed to shout,

"SHUT UP!"

What would happen if she did? Would there be a shocked silence? Would she hear again the child whisper pleadingly, "Let me in. Please, let me in!"

She wished she had the courage to try it. Then a better idea occurred to her. One of the doors on the landing was half open, and on the wall she saw a roll of lavatory paper, its end swinging gently in the draught.

"Excuse me," she said, and before they could stop her, darted in, and shut and locked the door.

Silence. And the whisper again, pleading, "Let me in! I promise I'll be good. Please let me in."

She looked round, puzzled, a little afraid.

"Where are you?" she asked. Outside the door, she could hear the muffled sound of voices, still talking as if they hoped to drown out the small voice. But the door was too thick.

"Let me in! Won't you let me in?" a child whispered.

Jane put down the seat and, kneeling on it, looked out of the window. The garden below was empty. There was no one perched in the branches of the nearby trees. A small wind, like a sigh, blew through the open window, and she shivered.

Still the voice pleaded, "Let me in! Let me in!"

When Jane came out, Charlotte was waiting for her on the landing. She was alone. The false animation had left her face. She looked pale and tired.

"So now you know," she said.

Close by, a child whispered incessantly, "Let me in! Let me in!"

"Where is it?" Jane asked nervously.

Charlotte shrugged. "In the house. In the garden. Not outside the walls, thank heavens! It doesn't do anything. Just whispers. On and on and on till we could scream. We turn the radio up loud, or the telly – the whole house shakes with noise and our heads ache, and still we know it's there. Even in my sleep I hear it, knocking softly on my head, asking to be let in. I *hate* it!"

"Why don't you move house?" Jane asked.

"You don't understand," Charlotte said. "We didn't find it here. We brought it with us. It's ours."

"Let me in. Please let me in," the child whispered. "I want to play with you."

They went to the park after all, running all the way there, racing away from the sound of a radio turned up too loud and a child's whisper. It was quiet in the park. There were not many people about. Most of the children had already gone home to supper. An old lady was throwing slices of bread from a wrapped loaf into the pond. The ducks pecked at it half-heartedly.

"They used to take her to feed the ducks," Charlotte said. "It wasn't as if they were horrid to her."

"Who?"

"My father's little sister. Mary. She'd have been my aunt if she'd lived. I don't know if you can be an aunt if you're already dead, do you?"

Nearby, some boys were kicking a ball about on the grass. They had put some sweaters down to mark a goal mouth, and they cheered as the ball went sailing through. As it bounced off the ground, a little girl ran forward to catch it, and missed. It slipped through her fingers and hit her cheek. She began to cry.

"It's yer own fault," an older boy said roughly. "Why didn't yer stay at 'ome like I told yer to?"

"I wanna play," the little girl whined. "I wanna play with yer, Mike."

"It must have been like that," Charlotte said, watching the little girl. "I wonder if her name is Mary, too. If so, those boys had better watch out."

"What happened?" Jane asked.

"Nothing much! That's what's so unfair," Charlotte said angrily. "She was too young, that's all. Dad was eight when she was born, and Uncle Peter and Uncle Mark even older. There'd just been the three of them before, you see."

"Didn't they want a baby sister?"

"I don't know. I don't suppose they minded," Charlotte said, shrugging. "Dad said they quite liked her when she was in her pram. Or tucked up in her cot with her teddy bear. It was when she could walk, that's when the trouble started. She was always tagging after them, wanting to play."

The little girl in the park was sitting on the ground now, sucking her thumb. Her eyes followed the ball longingly.

"Didn't they let her? I mean, not ever?" Jane asked.

"Yes! Sometimes. They weren't horrid to her. But – well, Dad said Mary was so clumsy. She always fell down and hurt herself, and they'd be blamed. She couldn't climb trees. She couldn't play cricket. Three of her front teeth were knocked out once. Dad said she just stood there, watching the ball coming, and didn't even have the sense to duck. It was only her milk teeth, but they got into a terrible row."

"Did they begin to hate her then?" Jane asked.

"*No!* They never *hated* her! They just didn't want her around all the time. When they were in their room, they'd bolt the door. They'd hear her outside, wailing, 'Let me in! Please let me in!' and they'd shout at her to go away. You can't blame them. She always broke their things. She didn't mean to, and she'd be sorry and cry."

"Poor Mary," Jane said, remembering the forlorn whisper. "I expect she was lonely."

"Don't take her side!" Charlotte said sharply. "Suppose she was sorry? Tears don't mean anything, do they? How'd you like *her* hanging around you all the time?" She gestured towards the little girl in front of them. "Would you like her following us everywhere, butting in, breaking our things?"

The little girl was standing up again, scratching her leg and sniffing. Then she started running after the ball. A boy charged into her, knocking her over.

"Mike, 'e 'urt me! Mike!" she wailed, but her brother took no notice.

"She shouldn't have got in the way," Charlotte said, and

Jane did not know which child she meant, the living or the dead.

"What happened in the end?" she asked.

"There was a terrible quarrel. My father had been making a model aeroplane, a big one. He'd spent weeks on it, and it was nearly finished. It was a beauty, he said. He was very proud of it. He couldn't lock his door. The key was lost. But he'd warned Mary that she must never, never go into his room when he was out, or something horrible would happen to her . . ."

"And she did?"

"Yes. He came back from school one day and found her sitting on the floor, crying, with all the broken pieces around her. 'I'm mending it for you, Johnny,' she said, looking frightened. 'I'm putting it together again.' He lost his temper. You can't blame him. Anyone would have done. He pushed her from the room, shouting at the top of his voice, 'Get out and stay out! Don't come near me again as long as you live! I hate you!'" Charlotte was silent for a moment; then she said stubbornly, "You can't blame him."

"No," Jane agreed.

"She was taken ill that night, and rushed to hospital. He never saw her again. They said she was too weak for visitors. And she died. She just seemed to fade away. It was nothing to do with him. But he thought it was his fault. It was then the whispering started."

It was still quite early when they came back from the park,

only half past six. The warm evening sunlight polished the green door till it shone like an emerald.

"Don't go yet," Charlotte begged. "Stay a bit longer."

Jane hesitated. The atmosphere of the hidden house, the over-loud voices and the frantic laughter remained in her mind like a bad taste. And the small voice whispering . . . *Poor little girl*, she thought, and shivered.

"People never want to come again," Charlotte said bitterly. "They're interested, they want to hear all about it, but suddenly they don't want to know us any more. It's as if we had the plague."

"I'm not scared," Jane said untruthfully. "I'll come in. I don't have to be back yet."

Charlotte's face brightened. She opened the door with a key, saying slyly, "No need to warn them now, since you've found out. Let's stay out in the garden and talk. I'll just tell them we're back." And she ran off into the house, leaving Jane alone.

Jane walked idly over the lawn, looking unseeingly at the flowers, her mind full of what she'd heard. She stepped on something that rolled beneath her foot, nearly unbalancing her. Looking down, she saw it was an old tennis ball, nearly as green as the grass. She picked it up and began tossing it into the air and catching it again . . .

"Let me in," the child whispered. "Please let me in."

Jane swung round, her heart racing. She had thought she was safe in the garden. Slowly she began backing towards the wall.

"Go away!" she said fiercely.

"Let me in," the child implored. "I'll be good. I promise I'll be good." It was such a piteous sound, the voice of a child who had been crying in the dark too long, that it touched Jane's heart. She could not send it away.

"I want to play with you," the child whispered. "Please let me play with you."

"Where are you?"

"Here."

"Catch!" Jane threw the tennis ball in the air. It fell unchecked and bounced across the grass. *I've gone mad*, she thought, watching it. But then there was a sound of quick, excited breathing, and the voice said, "I'll get it! I'll get it!"

Jane saw the ball rise up from the ground and hang in the air like a stained moon. Then it came sailing towards her, a feeble throw that would have fallen short, had she not raced forwards and scooped it up, her knuckles grazing the grass.

"Where are you?" she asked again.

"Here."

She tossed the ball to where the voice had seemed to come from, and saw it stop suddenly, caught in invisible hands.

"Well done!" she cried, and heard the child laugh gleefully.

Jane was suddenly filled with wild excitement. All her fear was gone, replaced by a strange joy. "Throw it again!" she called. "Let's have a game!"

The ball flew towards her, a high, arching shot. Before she could jump for it, a hand reached over her head and caught it. Startled, she looked round.

Three tall men stood behind her, Charlotte's father and her two uncles. Behind them, Jane saw her friend, coming slowly over the grass, her eyes wide and nervous. It was Charlotte's father who had caught the ball. Jane noticed for the first time, now that he was no longer talking and laughing, how tired he looked. There were deep lines on his forehead and round his mouth.

"Hullo, Mary," he said softly, looking over Jane's head to the empty grass, as if he longed to see someone standing there. His face seemed to waver, as if it were a reflection in disturbed water. The lines of age became bars through which a boy's face looked out pleadingly.

"Can we play too?" he asked, almost timidly, and tossed the ball gently in the air. It came back so fast that he missed it, and the invisible child squealed with laughter, calling out, "Butterfingers! Who's butterfingers now?"

A strange game began on the sunlit lawn, three men and two girls running and leaping and shouting, playing with a ghost child they could hear, but could not see. Her cries rang out in the evening air, sweet as a bird.

"Here I am! Not there, silly! Missed again!"

And the three middle-aged men ran about like boys shouting, "Over here! Jump for it! Oh, well done, Mary! Did you see that catch?"

At last, out of breath, they stopped. The ball fell to the grass and rolled slowly away.

The child said, "I've got to go now. Time for bed. You're not cross with me any more, are you, Johnny?"

Charlotte's father said gently, "No, Mary. I'm not cross, little sister. Go to your sleep."

The voice was further away when it spoke again. Very soft, very joyful.

"Goodnight," it said. "Goodnight, goodnight!"

Then there was silence. Nobody spoke. Jane and Charlotte and the three men stood still as statues. Leaves shifted in the wind above their heads. A bird called from a tree. Some gardens away, someone was pushing a lawnmower backwards and forwards. It was a beautiful summer evening, washed by a golden sun.

"I'd forgotten," Charlotte's father said, and though his voice was unsteady, he was smiling. "Poor little monkey-face, she never could go to sleep till we'd made it up. I'd forgotten that."

# TEXTS

## URSULA LE GUIN

MESSAGES CAME, JOHANNA thought, usually years too late, or years before one could crack their code or had even learned the language they were in. Yet they came increasingly often and were so urgent, so compelling in their demand that she read them, that she do something, as to force her at last to take refuge from them. She rented, for the month of January, a little house with no telephone in a seaside town that had no mail delivery. She had stayed there several times in summer; winter, as she had hoped, was even quieter than summer. A whole day would go by without her hearing or speaking a word. She did not buy the paper or turn on the television, and the one morning she thought she ought to find some news on the radio she got a programme in Finnish from Astoria. But the messages still came. Words were everywhere.

Literate clothing was no real problem. She remembered the first print dress she had ever seen, years ago, a genuine *print* dress with typography involved in the design – green on white, suitcases and hibiscus and the names *Riviera* and *Capri* and *Paris* occurring rather blobbily from shoulder-seam to hem, sometimes right side up, sometimes upside down. Then it had been, as the saleswoman said, very unusual. Now it was hard to find a T-shirt that did not urge political action, or quote lengthily from a dead physicist, or at least mention the town it was for sale in. All this she had coped with, she had even worn. But too many things were becoming legible.

She had noticed in earlier years that the lines of foam left by waves on the sand after stormy weather lay sometimes in curves that looked like handwriting, cursive lines broken by spaces, as if in words; but it was not until she had been alone for over a fortnight and had walked many times down to Wreck Point and back that she found she could read the writing. It was a mild day, nearly windless, so that she did not have to march briskly but could mosey along between the foam-lines and the water's edge where the sand reflected the sky. Every now and then a quiet winter breaker driving up and up the beach would drive her and a few gulls ahead of it onto the drier sand; then as the wave receded she and the gulls would follow it back. There was not another soul on the long beach. The sand lay as firm and even as a pad of pale brown paper, and on it a recent wave at its high mark had left a complicated series of curves and bits of foam. The ribbons and loops and lengths of white looked so much like handwriting in chalk that she stopped, the way she would stop, half willingly, to read what people scratched in the sand in summer. Usually it was "Jason + Karen" or paired initials in a heart; once, mysteriously and memorably, three initials and the dates 1973-1984, the only such inscription that spoke of a promise not made but broken. Whatever those eleven years had been – the length of a marriage? a child's life? – they were gone, and the letters and numbers also were gone when she came back by where they had been, with the tide rising. She had wondered then if the person who wrote them had written them to be erased. But these foam words lying on the brown sand now had been written by the erasing sea itself. If she could read them they might tell her a wisdom a good deal deeper and bitterer than she could possibly swallow. *Do I want to know what the sea writes?* she thought, but at the same time she was already reading the foam, which though in vaguely cuneiform blobs rather than letters of any alphabet was perfectly legible as she walked along beside it. "Yes," it read, "esse hes hetu tokye to' ossusess ekyes. Seham hute' u." (When she wrote it down later she used the apostrophe to represent a kind of stop or click like the last sound in "Yep!") As she read it over, backing up some yards to do so, it continued to say the same thing, so she walked up and down it several times and memorized it. Presently, as bubbles burst and the blobs began to shrink, it changed here and there to read, "Yes, e hes etu kye to' ossusess kye. ham te u." She felt that this was not significant change but mere loss, and kept the original text in mind. The water of the foam sank into the sand and the bubbles dried away till the marks and lines lessened into a faint lacework of dots and scraps, half legible. It looked enough like delicate bits of fancywork that she wondered if one could also read lace or crochet.

When she got home she wrote down the foam words so that she would not have to keep repeating them to remember them, and then she looked at the machine made Quaker lace tablecloth on the little round dining table. It was not hard to read but was, as one might expect, rather dull. She made out the first line inside the border as "pith wot pith wot pith wot" interminably, with a "dub" every thirty stitches where the border pattern interrupted.

But the lace collar she had picked up at a second-hand clothes store in Portland was a different matter entirely. It was handmade, hand-written. The script was small and very even. Like the Spencerian hand she had been taught fifty years ago in the first grade, it was ornate but surprisingly easy to read. "My soul must go," was the border, repeated many times, "my soul must go, my soul must go," and the fragile webs leading inward read, "sister, sister, sister, light the light." And she did not know what she was to do, or how she was to do it.

# THE SKY SEA
## HELEN CRESSWELL

YOU DON'T HAVE to believe this story. Plenty wouldn't. I'm just telling you what happened, that's all. In fact, I may as well tell you that the main reason I'm writing it all down is in the hope that once I see it in black and white, *I* won't believe it, either. If there is one thing I don't want, it's to end up like my great aunt Cass. I'm hoping to be a neurosurgeon.

I know perfectly well that nobody has great aunts these days, but I did. (Past tense, you notice.) I'm an only, so when I was little my parents were always farming me out to relatives so that I'd get the feeling of belonging to a big, happy family. Some chance. All my aunts and uncles, and particularly my cousins, are horrendous. One of them even has personalized plates on his car, for heaven's sake. One of the main things I'm looking forward to about being grown-up is being able to ditch the lot of them. So it's rather sad that the one person I did like visiting was Great Aunt Cass.

She was what my mother called "slightly dotty", but was probably just plain mad. You'll be able to make your own mind up. But the point is that when I was little, my favourite thing was going to stay with her.

# THE SKY SEA

She lived in a tiny village in Herefordshire called Flintham. Her house was very old and full of odd shadows and corners – rather like its owner, I suppose. It had a funny smell – of herbs, I think. She was always growing them and drying them. I used to help her, and she'd tell me what they all were and what ills they cured. I can't remember any of them, and in any case doubt whether they'll come in for much when I'm a neurosurgeon. Anyway, she believed in them all right, and used to call the local GP "Dr Quack" – sometimes to his face. I thought it was his real name, at the time.

The minute my parents had driven off Great Aunt Cass would fix me with her eye and grin the wickedest grin I've ever seen on any old lady.

"Well, Daisy dear, what shall we do for treats?"

And I'd shake my head and say, "You choose," because I knew I'd never be able to think up anything half as good as what she'd come up with. A lot of her treats were to do with eats. We'd make a whole batch of macaroons or drop scones and scoff the lot in a sitting. Or we'd catch a bus into Ledbury and go to this café where we'd have two cream teas each, one after the other. My parents would have gone spare if they'd known. They were keen on healthy eating as well as big families. I was only allowed one biscuit a day at home.

Then we'd go looking for watercress. Great Aunt Cass would wear these old wellies and tuck her skirts right up, and once she even fell over in the stream and got soaked, which was marvellous. She didn't even care. She just squelched home and got changed and swallowed a great steaming mug full of some herb tea. Most old ladies I know would have gone into a galloping decline, even supposing they'd have gone wading about looking for watercress in the first place. I don't know how old she was, but at the time I thought she must be about a hundred.

If it rained we used to cut out these old Victorian cards and pictures she had and stick them on to cupboard doors and things as decorations. Or we'd make things she called "peas in a pod". This meant that we'd each make exactly the same thing – a cat in clay, for instance, or a cardboard stand-up doll to dress. They never came out like peas in a pod, of course, but she said it didn't matter.

"You've got one, and I've got one. It's a charm – it binds us together."

I liked the idea of that. One day, she said, "We'll make something together, and then we'll split it in half. Half for you and half for me. That will bind us even closer."

So we made a big bird, a swallow, out of clay. And while it was still soft, she cut it straight down the middle with a knife. Then when it was baked we had half each and painted it blue. She kept her half on the mantelpiece, and I took mine home and kept it by the side of my bed.

"That's *real* magic," she said.

I told you she was mad.

I can't remember exactly how old I was when she first started talking about the sea in the sky. I think I must have been around five or six. However old I was, I sure as hell believed every single word of it.

# THE SKY SEA

Oh Lord. I can see that when I start telling it you're going to think I'm totally off my trolley. What you've got to remember is that although I'm fifteen now, I was only *little*. In fact, what I think I'll do, if you don't mind, is from now on tell it as if it were a story in the third person – Daisy said this, Daisy did that, and so on. That way you'll get the message that it was me then, not me now. I mean, it could just as well have happened to you. I didn't ask for it to happen, it just did.

Anyway, that's what I'll do. I may not tell it all that brilliantly – I never get all that good marks for English (unlike maths, physics, biology and chemistry, says she modestly). And from now on I'll just put GAC, instead of the whole mouthful (or penful), if you don't mind. So here goes . . .

Daisy was not very high and was in a forest world of gooseberries and blackcurrants. The smell was hot and sweet and dusty all at once. Her fingers were stained with juice but not her mouth, because you couldn't eat gooseberries and blackcurrants as fast as you picked them, as you could with raspberries and strawberries. You had to wait until they had been stewed into a lovely sweet sticky mixture that GAC called pot-pourri.

Winding in and out of the bushes was the ginger, white and tortoiseshell cat called Porker, though nobody knew why. If GAC were ever asked she simply replied, "It suits him." The sun beat down on Daisy and her bowl was nearly full. She thought of the home-made lemonade in the pantry, in a jug covered with muslin edged with beads. (She and GAC had made one each the day before.) She pushed through the jungle of leaves and out on to the square patch of grass. There was GAC, lying back in her chair gazing up at the sky. She didn't look at Daisy but she must have known she was there because she said, "Did you know there's a sea up there?"

Daisy, interested, put down her bowl and tilted back her head, screwing her eyes against the sun.

"A sea with tides and waves and ships and sailors."

Daisy squinted the harder. The sky was a fierce blue and flecked with wispy clouds, like foam. She shook her head.

"That's the sky," she said. She knew that for a fact.

"And above the sky, a sea." GAC's voice was far away and dreamy. It often was. "I know. Do you believe in mermaids?"

"Course," said Daisy promptly. It was a silly question.

"Of course. Sit here on the grass – lie down, if you like. And watch the sky – watch it very carefully."

Daisy obeyed. She lay on the hot grass and stared up, straining for a glimpse of a galleon with white sails, like the one in her nursery rhyme book. She was just on the point of thinking she saw one when she fell asleep.

"Well?" asked GAC when Daisy awoke. "Did you see anything?"

"I kind of did," replied Daisy. "Sort of."

Now she knew about the sea above the sky she would look up at the sky from time to time and see it with new eyes. It certainly looked deep enough to hold a sea.

It might have been that night, or the night after, or even the night after that when GAC told Daisy the story. She was always telling stories and they were marvellous ones about dragons and sorcerers and spells and they were all true.

"All the things I'm going to tell you really happened," she began that night. "And they happened many years ago, here in Flintham."

"Like the one about the man with two heads, you mean?"

"Precisely," said GAC. "Now don't interrupt. The story begins one thick, cloudy day – a Sunday, because the people were just coming out of church. All of them were thinking about their roast dinners, I daresay, just as you or I would. And then somebody noticed an anchor hanging on one of the tombstones."

"Which one? Not the one for Daisy Martha Bell in her seventieth year Life's Work Well Done?"

"Probably. It doesn't matter. The point is, anchors don't belong in churchyards, and this particular one certainly hadn't been there when they went in. They all crowded round to look, and saw that the anchor was attached to a cable, and that cable was pulled tight and stretching right into the sky as far as you could see. It just hung there in the air. It had them all by their ears, I can tell you! They gabbled and gawped and couldn't think what to do. And then the rope began to jerk and tug, right under their eyes, as if someone was trying to pull it up. But the anchor was hooked fast to the tombstone and wouldn't budge.

"Far away up above the congregation could hear voices shouting, and then they knew that up there, although it was quite impossible, was a ship, and sailors!

"And then – a sailor came sliding down the rope —"

"Out of the *sky*?"

"Out of the sky. He slid right down till he reached the ground, then seized the anchor and tugged and heaved to free it from the tombstone. But the anchor held fast. In the end he loosened it slightly, but just as he did so the villagers ran forward and seized him. They pulled him away from the anchor and held him down. After a while the sailors above must have given up hope, because the cable was cut and came spiralling down out of the sky and fell in a huge heap."

"Oh, the poor man! And he couldn't get back."

"He couldn't get back. He died. He drowned, I suppose you might say."

"Poor man, poor man!"

"And his ship in the sky went sailing away without him."

"What was it like?"

"The ship? No one knows. No one saw it."

"Perhaps there wasn't one at all."

"You can't have an anchor without a ship."

"And it's all true?"

"True as I sit here with my shoes pinching. Wait till tomorrow and I'll show you something."

The next day Daisy went with GAC to the church. Porker went paddling after them through the long grass. He always did, just like a dog. Daisy looked left and right among the barnacled tombstones for sign of an anchor.

"Not today," GAC told her. "Anchors never drop in the same place twice."

Then she led Daisy to the thick oak door of the church and pointed at the great iron hinges.

"The anchor!" she said. "The people forged those hinges out of the anchor, in memory of that amazing event."

Gingerly Daisy touched them, first one, then the other. They were cold – sea cold.

Now that she knew for certain that there was a sea above the sky, Daisy soon began to take it for granted. She even supposed that rain was that same sea, leaking. Before, she had wondered wherever it could come from. Now the world made more sense.

After that, on every visit GAC would talk about the sea in the sky. She had seen the ships, she said. They were tall-masted with billowing white sails. She had heard the sailors singing aloft.

"I suppose that to them, all earth folk are mermaids," mused GAC. "You and I are mermaids, dear."

Daisy looked dubiously down at her shoes and socks, but said nothing.

Then one time – it must have been a summer or two later – GAC showed Daisy a curious curved comb, carved out of tortoiseshell. It looked very old and had a pale, misty bloom.

"I found it among the hollyhocks," she said. "It must have been dropped over the side of a ship!"

"So it must," agreed Daisy.

She ran straight into the garden to see if she could find something of her own. She poked among the pansies and delphiniums and in among the raspberry cane forest, but all she found was a rusty teaspoon.

"Mine," GAC told her. "Not old – just rusty. Never mind. Just wait."

By now Daisy was so certain that she lived at the bottom of a real sea, that she half expected to see fishes fly instead of birds, coral for stones, silvery sand for earth. Ghostly galleons wove in and out of her dreams.

On Daisy's next visit GAC began to talk about going away.

"It's a secret, between you and me," she told Daisy.

"You won't go forever?" Daisy didn't like people to disappear. She didn't like the way GAC disappeared between visits and would make her write letters to prove that she was still there.

"That I can't tell. I am going on a voyage."

"On a ship?"

"On a ship."

"On the sea above the sky?"

"You guessed," GAC told her.

"But how will you get up there? Will you climb up a rope?"

"I don't know that, either. But I expect the sailors will haul me up. Me and Porker."

"*Porker?*"

"He shall be ship's cat. He'll like it. I think he was born to be a ship's cat. Haven't you noticed the way he rolls as he goes, like a sailor?"

Daisy hadn't. She thought that Porker walked in a perfectly ordinary cat-like way. If anything was strange about him, it was his name.

"My throat feels sore," she said. She said it to change the subject, because she didn't want to think about GAC and Porker sailing off in the sky, but it was true anyway.

Soon her throat was so sore that she couldn't swallow, and her arms and legs didn't seem to want to move. She remembered being put to bed and the doctor being there. She remembered GAC wiping her face with something damp and cool, giving her something sweet and sticky, and then something cold and slippery to swallow. It was night, and the curtains were undrawn as they always were. And it was the longest and strangest night Daisy had ever known.

Afterwards she could never sort out what were dreams and what were memories. All she knew was that that night both she and GAC saw a galleon sail right over the moon in a smoking sea of cloud. GAC threw open the window, and in, on the cold draught, there blew the faint and faraway shouts of sailors.

"They're there, my darling," said the voice of GAC. "Don't you hear them?"

But Daisy was herself adrift on a fathomless sea and did not answer, though she followed the wake of the ship with her eyes and thought she heard gulls crying.

Next day when she opened her eyes Daisy looked straight at the sky, but it had closed again, gone ordinary, and the ship had gone.

"You had a fever," GAC told her. "But you'll mend, and not on account of Dr Quack, either. You can take his sticky medicine but it's mine'll put you to rights."

So Daisy obediently swallowed both, and did mend, though she never knew which to thank.

She was still wobbly on the day she went home.

"Goodbye," said GAC. "Look out for Porker and me in the sky."

"Oh, you will come back, say you'll come back!"

"Make no promises you can't keep," replied GAC. "But I promise you one thing. I'll send you a sign. And I'll give you this to keep."

She opened her hand and there was the old curved comb with its curious milky bloom.

"Oh, *thank* you!"

It would go beside her bed, with the blue half-swallow.

"And not a word!"

"Promise!"

Daisy said goodbye to GAC and to Porker, and never saw either of them again.

"She says she's gone on a voyage," Daisy's mother said, when the letter came. "I suppose she means a cruise. At her age! Oh well, she always was slightly dotty. Oh – and taken Porker, she says!"

"That's more than slightly dotty," said Daisy's father. "That's trouble."

"Oh, she can't possibly have taken him. They wouldn't allow it. I expect she's put him in a home."

As the weeks passed, no postcards arrived from foreign parts. Daisy, of course, did not expect any, since she thought it unlikely that there was a post office in the sky. She kept her eyes glued to that sky and sometimes wondered, when her eyes began to ache, whether perhaps this was a different sky from the one that hung over Flintham.

"We had better go over and see what's happening," Daisy's mother said one day.

The garden was already overgrown. Soon, thought Daisy, the raspberries and gooseberries and thistles could close up in a thicket, as if in a fairytale. On the back door was pinned a note, by now faded and smudged by sun and rain. "Gone on a voyage. Don't know when I'll be back."

Enquiries were made in the village.

"Oh yes, Miss Norton said she was going on a voyage."

"A cruise, you mean?"

"That's not what she said. She said a voyage, I'm sure. And that's what the note on her door says."

And that was that. There was nothing more to be done. And Daisy kept her secret.

So there you are. Now do you see why I wanted to tell it in the third person? It's odd – as I was telling it, it all came back very clearly – I could even smell things – the hot blackcurrants, the warm macaroons, the scent of herbs. But Daisy Then doesn't seem to be Daisy Now at all. I can hardly believe I was her, once. Imagine believing all that guff!

The only thing is, I haven't quite told you everything. I don't really want to, but I know I must, or it would be cheating. And it's the real reason I'm telling the story at all.

It happened last week. I swear I hadn't been thinking about

GAC at all. In fact the only time I ever think of her now is when I see that half-swallow and the comb. I was in the garden, revising, and absolutely *compos mentis*. Then all of a sudden, right out of the blue, I thought I heard GAC's voice, "Ahoy! Daisy!" That's all – and then a soft thud, right nearby. Believe it or not, I actually looked up at the sky, and of course there was nothing there. But then I looked down. And there, quite close by, was something blue and shiny. It was the other half of that clay swallow we'd made together that rainy day, all those years ago in Flintham.

# THE ADVENTURE OF THE SUSSEX VAMPIRE

## SIR ARTHUR CONAN DOYLE

HOLMES HAD READ carefully a note which the last post had brought him. Then, with the dry chuckle which was his nearest approach to a laugh, he tossed it over to me.

"For a mixture of the modern and the medieval, of the practical and of the wildly fanciful, I think this is surely the limit," said he. "What do you make of it, Watson?" I read as follows:

> 46 OLD JEWRY
> Nov. 19th
>
> *Re* Vampires
>
> SIR,
>
> Our client, Mr Robert Ferguson, of Ferguson and Muirhead, tea brokers, of Mincing Lane, has made some inquiry from us in a communication of even date concerning vampires. As our firm specializes entirely upon the assessment of machinery the matter hardly comes without our purview, and we have therefore recommended Mr Ferguson to call upon you and lay the matter before you. We have not forgotten your successful action in the case of Matilda Briggs.
>
> We are, Sir, faithfully yours,

# MYSTIFYING

MORRISON, MORRISON AND DODD
per E.J.C.

"Matilda Briggs was not the name of a young woman, Watson," said Holmes in a reminiscent voice. "It was a ship which is associated with the giant rat of Sumatra, a story for which the world is not yet prepared. But what do we know about vampires? Does it comes within our purview either? Anything is better than stagnation, but really we seem to have been switched on to a Grimm's fairytale. Make a long arm, Watson, and see what V has to say."

I leaned back and took down the great index volume to which he referred. Holmes balanced it on his knee and his eyes moved slowly and lovingly over the record of old cases, mixed with the accumulated information of a lifetime.

"Voyage of the *Gloria Scott,*" he read. "That was a bad business. I have some recollection that you made a record of it, Watson, though I was unable to congratulate you upon the result. Victor Lynch, forger. Venomous lizard or gila. Remarkable case, that! Vittoria, the circus belle. Vanderbilt and the Yeggman. Vipers, Vogir, the Hammersmith wonder. Hullo! Hullo! Good old index. You can't beat it. Listen to this, Watson. Vampirism in Hungary. And again, Vampires in Transylvania." He turned over the pages with eagerness, but after a short intent perusal he threw down the great book with a snarl of disappointment.

"Rubbish, Watson, rubbish! What have we to do with walking corpses who can only be held in their grave by stakes driven through their hearts? It's pure lunacy."

"But surely," said I, "the vampire was not necessarily a dead man? A living person might have the habit. I have read for example, of the old sucking the blood of the young in order to retain their youth."

"You are right, Watson. It mentions the legend in one of these references. But are we to give serious attention to such things? This Agency stands flatfooted upon the ground, and there it must remain. The world is big enough for us. No ghosts need apply. I fear that we cannot take Mr Robert Ferguson very seriously. Possibly this note may be from him, and may throw some light upon what is worrying him."

He took up a second letter which had lain unnoticed upon the table whilst he had been absorbed with the first. This he began to read with a smile of amusement upon his face which gradually faded away into an expression of intense interest and concentration. When he had finished he sat for some little time lost in thought with the letter dangling from his fingers. Finally, with a start, he aroused himself from his reverie.

"Cheeseman's, Lamberley. Where is Lamberley, Watson?"

"It is in Sussex, south of Horsham."

"Not very far, eh? And Cheeseman's?"

"I know that country, Holmes. It is full of old houses which are named after the men who built them centuries ago. You get Odley's and Harvey's and Carriton's – the folk are forgotten but their names live in their houses."

"Precisely," said Holmes coldly. It was one of the peculiarities of his proud, self-contained nature that, though he docketed any fresh information very quickly and accurately in his brain, he seldom made any acknowledgement to the giver. "I rather fancy we shall know a good deal more about Cheeseman's, Lamberley, before we are through. The letter is, as I had hoped, from Robert Ferguson. By the way, he claims acquaintance with you."

"With me!"

"You had better read it."

He handed the letter across. It was headed with the address quoted.

DEAR MR HOLMES, [it said]

I have been recommended to you by my lawyers, but indeed the matter is so extraordinarily delicate that it is most difficult to discuss. It concerns a friend for whom I am acting. This gentleman married some five years ago a Peruvian lady, the daughter of a Peruvian merchant, whom he had met in connection with the importation of nitrates. The lady was very beautiful, but the fact of her foreign birth and of her alien religion always caused a separation of interests and of feelings between husband and wife, so that after a time his love may have cooled towards her and he may have come to regard their union as a mistake. He felt there were sides of her character which he could never explore or understand. This was the more painful as she was as loving a wife as a man could have – to all appearance absolutely devoted.

Now for the point which I will make more plain when we meet. Indeed, this note is merely to give you a general idea of the situation and to ascertain whether you would care to interest yourself in the matter. The lady began to show some curious traits quite alien to her ordinarily sweet and gentle disposition. The gentleman had been married twice and he had one son by the first wife. This boy was now fifteen, a very charming and affectionate youth, though unhappily injured through an accident in childhood. Twice the wife was caught in the act of assaulting this poor lad in the most unprovoked way. Once she struck him with a stick and left a great weal on his arm.

This was a small matter, however, compared with the conduct to her own child, a dear boy just under one year of age. On one occasion about a month ago this child had been left by its nurse for a few minutes. A loud cry from the baby, as of pain, called the nurse back. As she ran into the room she saw her employer, the lady, leaning over the baby and apparently biting his neck. There was a small wound in the neck, from which a stream of blood had escaped. The nurse was so horrified that she wished to call the husband, but the lady implored her not to do so, and actually gave her five pounds as a price for her silence. No explanation was ever given, and for the moment the matter was passed over.

It left, however, a terrible impression upon the nurse's mind, and from that time she began to watch her mistress closely, and to keep a closer guard upon the baby, whom she tenderly loved. It seemed to her that even as she watched the mother, so the mother watched her, and that every time she was compelled to leave the baby alone the mother was waiting to get at it. Day and night the nurse covered the child, and day and night the silent, watchful mother seemed to be lying in wait as a wolf waits for a lamb. It must read most incredible to you, and yet I beg you to take it seriously, for a child's life and a man's sanity may depend upon it.

At last there came one dreadful day when the facts could no longer be concealed from the husband. The nurse's nerve had given way; she could stand the strain no longer, and she made a clean breast of it all to the man. To him it seemed as wild a tale as it may now seem to you. He knew his wife to be a loving wife, and, save for the assaults upon her stepson, a loving mother. Why, then, should she wound her own dear little baby? He told the nurse that she was dreaming, that her suspicions were those of a lunatic, and that such libels upon her mistress were not to be tolerated. Whilst they were talking, a sudden cry of pain was heard. Nurse and master rushed together to the nursery. Imagine his feelings, Mr Holmes, as he saw his wife rise from a kneeling position beside the cot, and saw blood upon the child's exposed neck and upon the sheet. With a cry of horror, he turned his wife's face to the light and saw blood all round her lips. It was she – she beyond all question – who had drunk the poor baby's blood.

So the matter stands. She is now confined to her room. There has been no explanation. The husband is half demented. He knows, and I know, little of Vampirism beyond the name. We had thought it was some wild tale of foreign parts. And yet here in the very heart of English Sussex – well, all this can be discussed with you in the morning. Will you see me? Will you use your great powers in aiding a distracted man? If so, kindly wire to Ferguson, Cheeseman's, Lamberley, and I will be at your rooms by ten o'clock.

Yours faithfully,

ROBERT FERGUSON

PS – I believe your friend Watson played Rugby for Blackheath when I was three-quarter for Richmond. It is the only personal introduction which I can give.

"Of course I remember him," said I, as I laid down the letter. "Big Bob Ferguson, the finest three-quarter Richmond ever had. He was always a good-natured chap. It's like him to be so concerned over a friend's case."

Holmes looked at me thoughtfully and shook his head.

"I never get your limits, Watson," said he. "There are unexplored possibilities about you. Take a wire down, like a good fellow. 'Will examine your case with pleasure.'"

"Your case!"

"We must not let him think that this Agency is a home for the weak-minded. Of course it is his case. Send him that wire and let the matter rest till morning."

Promptly at ten o'clock next morning Ferguson strode into our room. I had remembered him as a long, slab-sided man with loose limbs and a fine turn of speed, which had carried him round many an opposing back. There is surely nothing in life more painful than to meet the wreck of a fine athlete whom one has known in his prime. His great frame had fallen in, his flaxen hair was scanty, and his shoulders were bowed. I fear that I roused corresponding emotions in him.

"Hullo, Watson," said he, and his voice was still deep and

hearty. "You don't look quite the man you did when I threw you over the ropes into the crowd at the Old Deer Park. I expect I have changed a bit also. But it's this last day or two that has aged me. I see by your telegram, Mr Holmes, that it is no use my pretending to be anyone's deputy."

"It is simpler to deal direct," said Holmes.

"Of course it is. But you can imagine how difficult it is when you are speaking of the one woman you are bound to protect and help. What can I do? How am I to go to the police with such a story? And yet the kiddies have got to be protected. Is it madness, Mr Holmes? Is it something in the blood? Have you any similar case in your experience? For God's sake, give me some advice, for I am at my wits' end."

"Very naturally, Mr Ferguson. Now sit here and pull yourself together and give me a few clear answers. I can assure you that I am far from being at my wits' end, and that I am confident we shall find some solution. First of all, tell me what steps you have taken. Is your wife still near the children?"

"We had a dreadful scene. She is a most loving woman, Mr Holmes. If ever a woman loved a man with all her heart and soul, she loves me. She was cut to the heart that I should have discovered this horrible, this incredible, secret. She would not even speak. She gave no answer to my reproaches, save to gaze at me with a wild, despairing look in her eyes. Then she rushed to her room and locked herself in. Since then she has refused to see me. She has a maid who was with her before her marriage, Dolores by name – a friend rather than a servant. She takes her food to her."

"Then the child is in no immediate danger?"

"Mrs Mason, the nurse, has sworn that she will not leave it night or day. I can absolutely trust her. I am more uneasy about poor little Jack, for, as I told you in my note, he has twice been assaulted by her."

"But never wounded?"

"No; she struck him savagely. It is the more terrible as he is a poor little inoffensive cripple." Ferguson's gaunt features softened as he spoke of his boy. "You would think that the dear lad's condition would soften anyone's heart. A fall in childhood and a twisted spine, Mr Holmes. But the dearest, most loving heart within."

Holmes had picked up the letter of yesterday and was reading it over. "What other inmates are there in your house, Mr Ferguson?"

"Two servants who have not been long with us. One stable-hand, Michael, who sleeps in the house. My wife, myself, my boy Jack, baby, Dolores and Mrs Mason. That is all."

"I gather that you did not know your wife well at the time of your marriage?"

"I had only known her a few weeks."

"How long had this maid Dolores been with her?"

"Some years."

"Then your wife's character would really be better known by Dolores than by you?"

"Yes, you may say so."

Holmes made a note.

"I fancy," said he, "that I may be of more use at Lamberley

than here. It is eminently a case for personal investigation. If the lady remains in her room, our presence could not annoy or inconvenience her. Of course, we would stay at the inn."

Ferguson gave a gesture of relief.

"It is what I hoped, Mr Holmes. There is an excellent train at two from Victoria, if you could come."

"Of course we could come. There is a lull at present. I can give you my undivided energies. Watson, of course, comes with us. But there are one or two points upon which I wish to be very sure before I start. This unhappy lady as I understand it, has appeared to assault both the children, her own baby, and your little son?"

"That is so."

"But the results take different forms, do they not? She has beaten your son."

"Once with a stick and once very savagely with her hands."

"Did she give no explanation why she struck him?"

"None, save that she hated him. Again and again she said so."

"Well, that is not unknown among stepmothers. A posthumous jealousy, we will say. Is the lady jealous by nature?"

"Yes, she is very jealous – jealous with all the strength of her fiery tropical love."

"But the boy – he is fifteen, I understand, and probably very developed in mind, since his body has been circumscribed in action. Did he give you no explanation of these assaults?"

"No; he declared there was no reason."

"Were they good friends at other times?"

"No; there was never any love between them."

"Yet you say he is affectionate?"

"Never in the world could there be so devoted a son. My life is his life. He is absorbed in what I say or do."

Once again Holmes made a note. For some time he sat lost in thought.

"No doubt you and the boy were great comrades before this second marriage. You were thrown very close together, were you not?"

"Very much so."

"And the boy, having so affectionate a nature, was devoted, no doubt, to the memory of his mother?"

"Most devoted."

"He would certainly seem to be a most interesting lad. There is one other point about these assaults. Were the strange attacks upon the baby and the assaults upon your son at the same period?"

"In her first case it was so. It was as if some frenzy had seized her, and she had vented her rage upon both. In the second case it was only Jack who suffered. Mrs Mason had no complaint to make about the baby."

"That certainly complicates matters."

"I don't quite follow you, Mr Holmes."

"Possibly not. One forms provisional theories and waits for time or fuller knowledge to explode them. A bad habit, Mr Ferguson; but human nature is weak. I fear that your old friend here has given an exaggerated view of my scientific methods.

However, I will only say at the present stage that your problem does not appear to me to be insoluble, and that you may expect to find us at Victoria at two o'clock."

It was evening of a dull, foggy November day when, having left our bags at The Chequers, Lamberley, we drove through the Sussex clay of a long winding lane, and finally reached the isolated and ancient farmhouse in which Ferguson dwelt. It was a large, straggling building, very old in the centre, very new at the wings, with towering Tudor chimneys and a lichen-spotted, high-pitched roof of Horsham slabs. The doorsteps were worn into curves, and the ancient tiles which lined the porch were marked with the rebus of a cheese and a man, after the original builder. Within, the ceilings were corrugated with heavy oaken beams, and the uneven floors sagged into sharp curves. An odour of age and decay pervaded the whole crumbling building.

There was one very large central room, into which Ferguson led us. Here, in a huge old-fashioned fireplace with an iron screen behind it dated 1670, there blazed and spluttered a splendid log fire.

The room, as I gazed round, was a most singular mixture of dates and of places. The half-panelled walls may well have belonged to the original yeoman farmer of the seventeenth century. They were ornamented, however, on the lower part by a line of well-chosen modern water-colours; while above, where yellow plaster took the place of oak, there was hung a fine collection of South American utensils and weapons, which had been brought, no doubt, by the Peruvian lady upstairs. Holmes rose, with that quick curiosity which sprang from his eager mind, and examined them with some care. He returned with his eyes full of thought.

"Hullo!" he cried. "Hullo!"

A spaniel had lain in a basket in the corner. It came slowly forward towards its master, walking with difficulty. Its hind-legs moved irregularly and its tail was on the ground. It licked Ferguson's hand.

"What is it, Mr Holmes?"

"The dog. What's the matter with it?"

"That's what puzzled the vet. A sort of paralysis. Spinal meningitis, he thought. But it is passing. He'll be all right soon – won't you, Carlo?"

A shiver of assent passed through the drooping tail. The dog's mournful eyes passed from one of us to the other. He knew that we were discussing his case.

"Did it come on suddenly?"

"In a single night."

"How long ago?"

"It may have been four months ago."

"Very remarkable. Very suggestive."

"What do you see in it, Mr Holmes?"

"A confirmation of what I had already thought."

"For God's sake, what do you think, Mr Holmes? It may be a mere intellectual puzzle to you, but it is life and death to me! My wife a would-be murderer – my child in constant danger! Don't play with me, Mr Holmes. It is too terribly serious."

The big rugby three-quarter was trembling all over. Holmes put his hand soothingly upon his arm.

"I fear that there is pain for you, Mr Ferguson, whatever the solution may be," said he. "I would spare you all I can. I cannot say more for the instant, but before I leave this house I hope I may have something definite."

"Please God you may! If you will excuse me, gentlemen, I will go up to my wife's room and see if there has been any change."

He was away some minutes, during which Holmes resumed his examination of the curiosities upon the wall. When our host returned it was clear from his downcast face that he had made no progress. He brought with him, a tall, slim girl.

"The tea is ready, Dolores," said Ferguson. "See that your mistress has everything she can wish."

"She verra ill," cried the girl, looking with indignant eyes at her master. "She no ask for food. She verra ill. She need doctor. I frightened stay alone with her without doctor."

Ferguson looked at me with a question in his eyes.

"I should be so glad if I could be of use."

"Would your mistress see Dr Watson?"

"I take him. I no ask leave. She needs doctor."

"Then I'll come with you at once."

I followed the girl, who was quivering with strong emotion, up the staircase and down an ancient corridor. At the end was an iron-clamped and massive door.

It struck me as I looked at it that if Ferguson tried to force his way to his wife he would find it no easy matter. The girl drew a key from her pocket, and the heavy oaken planks creaked upon their old hinges. I passed in and she swiftly followed, fastening the door behind her.

On the bed a woman was lying who was clearly in a high fever. She was only half conscious, but as I entered she raised a pair of frightened but beautiful eyes and glared at me in apprehension. Seeing a stranger, she appeared to be relieved, and sank back with a sigh upon the pillow. I stepped up to her with a few reassuring words, and she lay still while I took her pulse and temperature. Both were high, and yet my impression was the condition was rather that of mental and nervous excitement than of any actual seizure.

"She lie like that one day, two day. I 'fraid she die," said the girl.

The woman turned her flushed and handsome face towards me.

"Where is my husband?"

"He is below, and would wish to see you."

"I will not see him. I will not see him." Then she seemed to wander off into delirium. "A fiend! A fiend! Oh, what shall I do with this devil?"

"Can I help you in any way?"

"No. No one can help. It is finished. All is destroyed. Do what I will, all is destroyed."

The woman must have some strange delusion. I could not see honest Bob Ferguson in the character of fiend or devil.

"Madame," I said, "your husband loves you dearly. He is deeply grieved at this happening."

Again she turned on me those glorious eyes.

"He loves me. Yes. But do I not love him? Do I not love him even to sacrifice myself rather than break his dear heart? That is how I love him. And yet he could think of me – he could speak to me so."

"He is full of grief, but he cannot understand."

"No, he cannot understand. But he should trust."

"Will you not see him?" I suggested.

"No, no; I cannot forget those terrible words nor the look upon his face. I will not see him. Go now. You can do nothing for me. Tell him only one thing. I want my child. I have a right to my child. That is the only message I can send him." She turned her face to the wall and would say no more.

I returned to the room downstairs, where Ferguson and Holmes still sat by the fire. Ferguson listened moodily to my account of the interview.

"How can I send her the child?" he said. "How do I know what strange impulse might come upon her? How can I ever forget how she rose from beside it with its blood on her lips?" He shuddered at the recollection. "The child is safe with Mrs Mason, and there he must remain."

A smart maid, the only modern thing which we had seen in the house, had brought in some tea. As she was serving it the door opened and a youth entered the room. He was a remarkable lad, pale-faced and fair-haired, with excitable light blue eyes which blazed into a sudden flame of emotion and joy as they rested upon his father. He rushed forward and threw his arms round his neck with the abandon of a loving girl.

"Oh, Daddy," he cried. "I did not know that you were due yet. I should have been here to meet you. Oh, I am so glad to see you!"

Ferguson gently disengaged himself from the embrace with some little show of embarrassment.

"Dear old chap," said he, patting the flaxen head with a very tender hand. "I came early because my friends, Mr Holmes and Dr Watson, have been persuaded to come down and spend an evening with us."

"Is that Mr Holmes, the detective?"

"Yes."

The youth looked at us with a very penetrating and, as it seemed to me, unfriendly gaze.

"What about your other child, Mr Ferguson?" asked Holmes. "Might we make the acquaintance of the baby?"

"Ask Mrs Mason to bring baby down," said Ferguson. The boy went off with a curious, shambling gait which told my surgical eyes that he was suffering from a weak spine. Presently he returned, and behind him came a tall, gaunt woman bearing in her arms a very beautiful child, dark-eyed, golden-haired, a wonderful mixture of the Saxon and the Latin. Ferguson was evidently devoted to it, for he took it into his arms and fondled it most tenderly.

"Fancy anyone having the heart to hurt him," he muttered, as he glanced down at the small, angry red pucker upon the cherub throat.

It was at this moment that I chanced to glance at Holmes, and saw a most singular intentness in his expression. His face was as set as if it had been carved out of old ivory, and his eyes, which had glanced for a moment at father and child, were now fixed with eager curiosity upon something at the other side of the room. Following his gaze I could only guess that he was looking out through the window at the melancholy, dripping garden. It is true that a shutter had half closed outside and obstructed the view, but nonetheless it was certainly at the window that Holmes was fixing his concentrated attention. Then he smiled, and his eyes came back to the baby. On its chubby neck there was this small puckered mark. Without speaking, Holmes examined it with care. Finally he shook one of the dimpled fists which waved in front of him.

"Goodbye, little man. You have made a strange start in life. Nurse, I should wish to have a word with you in private."

He took her aside and spoke earnestly for a few minutes. I only heard the last words, which were: "Your anxiety will soon, I hope, be set at rest." The woman, who seemed to be a sour, silent kind of creature, withdrew with the child.

"What is Mrs Mason like?" asked Holmes.

"Not very prepossessing externally, as you can see, but a heart of gold, and devoted to the child."

"Do you like her, Jack?" Holmes turned suddenly upon the boy. His expressive mobile face shadowed over, and he shook his head.

"Jacky has very strong likes and dislikes," said Ferguson, putting his arm round the boy. "Luckily I am one of his likes."

The boy cooed and nestled his head upon his father's breast. Ferguson gently disengaged him.

"Run away, little Jacky," said he, and he watched his son with loving eyes until he disappeared. "Now, Mr Holmes," he continued, when the boy was gone. "I really feel that I have brought you on a fool's errand, for what can you possibly do, save give your sympathy? It must be an exceedingly delicate and complex affair from your point of view."

"It is certainly delicate," said my friend, with an amused smile, "but I have not been struck up to now with its complexity. It has been a case for intellectual deduction, but when this original intellectual deduction is confirmed point by point by quite a number of independent incidents, then the subjective becomes objective and we can say confidently that we have reached our goal. I had, in fact, reached it before we left Baker Street, and the rest has merely been observation and confirmation."

Ferguson put his big hand to his furrowed forehead.

"For heaven's sake, Holmes," he said hoarsely, "if you can see the truth in this matter, do not keep me in suspense. How do I stand? What shall I do? I care nothing as to how you have found your facts so long as you have really got them."

"Certainly I owe you an explanation, and you shall have it. But you will permit me to handle the matter in my own way? Is the lady capable of seeing us, Watson?"

"She is ill, but she is quite rational."

"Very good. It is only in her presence that we can clear the matter up. Let us go up to her."

"She will not see me," cried Ferguson.

"Oh, yes, she will," said Holmes. He scribbled a few lines upon a sheet of paper. "You at least have the *entrée*, Watson. Will you have the goodness to give the lady this note?"

I ascended again and handed the note to Dolores, who cautiously opened the door. A minute later I heard a cry from within, a cry in which joy and surprise seemed to be blended. Dolores looked out.

"She will see them. She will leesten," said she.

At my summons Ferguson and Holmes came up. As we entered the room Ferguson took a step or two towards his wife, who had raised herself in the bed, but she held out her hand to repulse him. He sank into an armchair, while Holmes seated himself beside him, after bowing to the lady, who looked at him with wide-eyed amazement.

"I think we can dispense with Dolores," said Holmes. "Oh, very well, madame, if you would rather she stayed I can see no objection. Now, Mr Ferguson, I am a busy man with many calls, and my methods have to be short and direct. The swiftest surgery is the least painful. Let me first say what will ease your mind. Your wife is a very good, a very loving, and a very ill-used woman."

Ferguson sat up with a cry of joy.

"Prove that, Mr Holmes, and I am your debtor for ever."

"I will do so, but in doing so I must wound you deeply in another direction."

"I care nothing so long as you clear my wife. Everything on earth is insignificant compared to that."

"Let me tell you, then, the train of reasoning which passed through my mind in Baker Street. The idea of a vampire was to me absurd. Such things do not happen in criminal practice in England. And yet your observation was precise. You had seen the lady rise from beside the child's cot with the blood upon her lips."

"I did."

"Did it not occur to you that a bleeding wound may be sucked for some other purpose than to draw the blood from it? Was there not a queen in English history who sucked such a wound to draw poison from it?"

"Poison!"

"A South American household. My instinct felt the presence of those weapons upon the wall before my eyes ever saw them. It might have been other poison, but that was what occurred to me. When I saw that little empty quiver beside the small bird-bow, it was just what I expected to see. If the child were pricked with one of those arrows dipped in curare or some other devilish drug, it would mean death if the venom were not sucked out.

"And the dog! If one were to use such a poison, would one not try it first in order to see that it had not lost its power? I did not foresee the dog, but at least I understood him and he fitted into my reconstruction.

"Now do you understand? Your wife feared such an attack. She saw it made and saved the child's life, and yet she shrank from telling you all the truth, for she knew how you loved the boy and feared lest it break your heart."

"Jacky!"

"I watched him as you fondled the child just now. His face was clearly reflected in the glass of the window where the shutter formed a background. I saw such jealousy, such cruel hatred, as I have seldom seen in a human face."

"My Jacky!"

"You have to face it, Mr Ferguson. It is the more painful because it is a distorted love, a maniacal exaggerated love for you, and possibly for his dead mother, which has prompted his action. His very soul is consumed with hatred for this splendid child, whose health and beauty are a contrast to his own weakness."

"Good God! It is incredible!"

"Have I spoken the truth, madame?"

The lady was sobbing, with her face buried in the pillows. Now she turned to her husband.

"How could I tell you, Bob? I felt the blow it would be to you. It was better that I should wait and that it should come from some other lips than mine. When this gentleman, who seems to have powers of magic, wrote that he knew all, I was glad."

"I think a year at sea would be my prescription for Master Jacky," said Holmes, rising from his chair. "Only one thing is still clouded, madame. We can quite understand your attacks upon Master Jacky. There is a limit to a mother's patience. But how did you dare to leave the child these last two days?"

"I had told Mrs Mason. She knew."

"Exactly. So I imagined."

Ferguson was standing by the bed, choking, his hands outstretched and quivering.

"This, I fancy, is the time for our exit, Watson," said Holmes in a whisper. "If you will take one elbow of the too faithful Dolores, I will take the other. There, now," he added, as he closed the door behind him, "I think we may leave them to settle the rest among themselves."

I have only one further note in this case. It is the letter which Holmes wrote in final answer to that with which the narrative begins. It ran thus:

BAKER STREET,

Nov. 21st

*Re* Vampires

SIR,

Referring to your letter of the 19th, I beg to state that I have looked into the inquiry of your client, Mr Robert Ferguson, of Ferguson and Muirhead, tea brokers, of Mincing Lane, and that the matter has been brought to a satisfactory conclusion. With thanks for your recommendation.

I am, Sir, faithfully yours,

SHERLOCK HOLMES

# THE BEWITCHED JACKET
## DINO BUZZATI

ALTHOUGH I APPRECIATE elegant dress, I don't usually pay attention to the perfection (or imperfection) with which my companions' clothing is cut.

Nonetheless, one night during a reception at a house in Milan, I met a man about forty years old who literally shone because of the simple and decisive beauty of his clothes.

I don't know who he was, I was meeting him for the first time, and at the introduction, as always happens, it was impossible to get his name. But at a certain point during the evening, I found myself near him, and we began to talk. He seemed a civil, well-bred man, but with an air of sadness. Perhaps with exaggerated familiarity – God should have stopped me – I complimented him on his elegance; and I even dared to ask him who his tailor might be.

He smiled curiously, as if he had expected my question.

"Nearly no one knows him," he said. "Still, he's a great master. And he works only when it comes to him. For a few initiates."

"So that I couldn't . . . ?"

"Oh, try, try. His name is Corticella, Alfonso Corticella, via

Ferrara 17."

"He will be expensive, I imagine."

"I believe so, but I swear I don't know. He made me this suit three years ago, and he still hasn't sent me the bill."

"Corticella? Via Ferrara 17, did you say?"

"Exactly," the stranger answered. And he left me to join another group of people.

At via Ferrara 17, I found a house like so many others and like those of so many other tailors; it was the residence of Alfonso Corticella. It was he who came to let me in. He was a little old man with black hair, which was, however, obviously dyed.

To my surprise, he was not hard to deal with. In fact, he seemed eager for me to be his customer. I explained to him how I had got his address, praised his cutting, and asked him to make me a suit. We selected a grey wool, then he took my measurements, and offered to come to my apartment for the fitting. I asked him the price. There was no hurry, he answered, we could always come to an agreement. What a congenial man, I thought at first. Nevertheless, later, while I was returning home, I realized that the little old man had left me feeling uneasy (perhaps because of his much too warm and persistent smiles). In short, I had no desire at all to see him again. But now the suit had been ordered. And after about three weeks it was ready.

When they brought it to me, I tried it on in front of a mirror for a little while. It was a masterpiece. Yet, I don't know why, perhaps because of my memory of the unpleasant old man, I didn't have any desire to wear it. And weeks passed before I decided to do so.

That day I shall remember forever. It was a Tuesday in April and it was raining. When I had slipped into the clothes – jacket, trousers, and vest – I was pleased to observe that they didn't pull and weren't tight anywhere, as almost always happens with new suits. And yet they wrapped me perfectly.

As a rule I put nothing in the right jacket pocket; in the left one, I keep my cards. This explains why, only after a couple of hours at the office, casually slipping my hand into the right pocket, I noticed that there was a piece of paper inside. Was it maybe the tailor's bill?

No. It was a ten thousand lire note.

I was astounded. I certainly had not put it there. On the other hand, it was absurd to think it a joke of the tailor Corticella. Much less did it seem a gift from my maid, the only person, other than the tailor, who had occasion to go near my suit. Or was it a counterfeit note? I looked at it in the light, I compared it to other ones. It couldn't be any better than these.

There was a single possible explanation: Corticella's absentmindedness. Perhaps a customer had come to make a payment. The tailor didn't have his wallet with him just then, and so to avoid leaving the money around, he slipped it into my jacket, which was hanging on a mannequin. These things can happen.

I rang for my secretary. I wanted to write a letter to Corticella, returning the money that was not mine. Yet (and I can't say why I did it) I slipped my hand into the pocket again.

"Is anything wrong, sir? Do you feel ill?" asked my secretary, who entered at that moment. I must have turned pale as death. In my pocket my fingers touched the edge of another strip of paper – which had not been there a few minutes before.

"No, no, it's nothing," I said. "A slight dizziness. It happens to me sometimes. Maybe I'm a little tired. You can go now, dear, I wanted to dictate a letter, but we'll do it later."

Only after my secretary had gone did I dare remove the piece of paper from my pocket. It was another ten thousand lire note. Then I tried a third time. And a third banknote came out.

My heart began to race. I had the feeling that for some mysterious reason I was involved in the plot of a fairytale, like those that are told to children and that no one believes are true.

On the pretext that I was not feeling well, I left the office and went home. I needed to be alone. Luckily, my maid had already gone. I shut the doors, lowered the blinds. I began to take out the notes one after another, very quickly. My pocket seemed inexhaustible.

I worked in a spasmodic nervous tension, with the fear that the miracle might stop at any moment. I wanted it to continue all day and night, until I had accumulated billions. But at a certain point the flow diminished.

Before me stood an impressive heap of banknotes. The important thing now was to hide them, so no one might get wind of the affair. I emptied an old trunk full of rugs and put the money, arranged in many little piles, at the bottom. The I slowly began counting. There were 58 million lire.

I awoke the next morning after the maid arrived. She was amazed to find me in bed still completely dressed. I tried to laugh, explaining that I had drunk a little too much the night before and sleep had suddenly seized me.

A new anxiety arose: she asked me to take off the suit, so she could at least give it a brushing.

I answered that I had to go out immediately and didn't have time to change. Then I hurried to a store selling ready-to-wear clothes to buy another suit made of a similar material; I would leave this one in the maid's care; "mine", the suit that in the course of a few days would make me one of the most powerful men in the world, I would hide in a safe place.

I didn't know whether I was living in a dream, whether I was happy or rather suffocating under the burden of too hard a fate. On the street, I was continually feeling the magic pocket through my raincoat. Each time I breathed a sigh of relief. Beneath the cloth answered the comforting crackle of paper money.

But a singular coincidence cooled my joyous delirium. News of a robbery that occurred the day before headlined the morning papers. A bank's armoured car, after making the rounds of the branches, was carrying the day's deposits to the main office when it was seized and cleaned out in viale Palmanova by four criminals. As people swarmed around the scene, one of the gangsters began to shoot to keep them away. A passerby was killed. But, above all, the amount of the loot struck me: it was exactly 58 million – like the money I had put in the trunk.

Could there be a connection between my sudden wealth and the criminal raid that happened almost simultaneously? It seemed foolish to think so. What's more, I am not superstitious. All the same, the incident left me very confused.

The more one gets, the more one wants. I was already rich, considering my modest habits. But the illusion of a life of unlimited luxury was compelling. And that same evening I set to work again. Now I proceeded more slowly, with less torture to my nerves. Another 135 million was added to my previous treasure.

That night I couldn't close my eyes. Was it the presentiment of danger? Or the tormented conscience of one who undeservedly wins a fabulous fortune? Or was it a kind of confused remorse? At dawn I leaped from the bed, dressed, and ran outside to get a newspaper.

As I read, I lost my breath. A terrible fire, which had begun in a naphtha warehouse, had half-destroyed a building on the main street, via San Cloro. The flames had consumed, among other things, the safes of a large real estate company which contained more than 130 million in cash. Two firemen met their deaths in the blaze.

Should I now, perhaps, list my crimes one by one? Yes, because now I knew that the money the jacket gave me came from those crimes, from blood, from desperation and death, from hell. But I was still within the snare of reason, which scornfully refused to admit that I was in any way responsible. And the temptation resumed, then the hand – it was so easy! slipped into the pocket, and the fingers, with the quickest delight, grasped the edges of always another banknote. The money, the divine money!

Without moving out of my old apartment (so as not to attract attention), I soon bought a huge villa, owned a precious collection of paintings, drove around in luxurious automobiles, and having left my firm for "reasons of health", travelled back and forth throughout the world in the company of marvellous women.

I knew that whenever I drew money from the jacket, something base and painful happened in the world. But it was still always a vague awareness, not supported by logical proofs. Meanwhile, at each new collection, my conscience was degraded, becoming more and more vile. And the tailor? I telephoned him to ask for the bill, but no one answered. In via Ferrara, when I went to search for him, they told me that he had emigrated abroad, they didn't know where. Everything then conspired to show me that without knowing it, I was bound in a pact with the Devil.

Until one morning, in the building where I lived for many years, they found a sixty-year-old retired woman asphyxiated by gas; she had killed herself for having mislaid her monthly pension of 30 thousand lire, which she had collected the day before (and which had ended up in my hands).

Enough, enough! In order not to sink to the depths of the abyss, I had to rid myself of the jacket. And not by surrendering it to someone else, because the horror would continue (who would ever be able to resist such enticement?). Its destruction was absolutely necessary.

By car I arrived at a secluded valley in the Alps. I left the car in a grassy clearing and set out in the direction of the forest. There wasn't a living soul in sight. Having gone beyond the forest, I reached the rocky ground of the moraine. Here, between two gigantic boulders, I pulled the wicked jacket from the knapsack, sprinkled it with kerosene, and lit it. In a few minutes only ashes were left.

But at the last flicker of the flames, behind me – it seemed about two or three metres away – a human voice resounded: "Too late, too late!" Terrified, I turned around with a serpent's snap. But I saw no one. I explored the area, jumping from one huge rock to another, to hunt out the damned person. Nothing. There were only rocks.

Notwithstanding the fright I experienced, I went back down to the base of the valley with a feeling of relief. I was free at last. And rich, luckily.

But my car was no longer in the grassy clearing. And after I returned to the city, my sumptuous villa had disappeared; in its place was an uncultivated field with some poles that bore the notice "Municipal Land For Sale". My saving accounts were also completely drained, but I couldn't explain how. The big packets of deeds in my numerous safe-deposit boxes had vanished too. And there was dust, nothing but dust, in the old trunk.

I now resumed working with difficulty, I hardly get

through a day, and what is stranger, no one seems to be amazed by my sudden ruin.

And I know that it's still not over, I know that one day my doorbell will ring. I'll answer it and find that cursed tailor before me, with his contemptible smile, asking for the final settling of my account.

# ACKNOWLEDGEMENTS

The publisher would like to thank the copyright holders for permission to reproduce the following copyright material:

**Joan Aiken**: A.M. Heath & Co. Ltd for "The Green Arches" by Joan Aiken. Copyright © Joan Aiken Enterprises Ltd 1996. **Vivien Alcock**: Reed Consumer Books Ltd for "The Whisperer" from *Ghostly Companions* by Vivien Alcock, Methuen Children's Books 1984. Copyright © Vivien Alcock 1984. **Ray Bradbury**: Don Congdon Associates Inc. for "The Scythe" from *The October Country* by Ray Bradbury. Copyright © Ray Bradbury 1956. **Dino Buzzati**: Carcanet Press for "The Bewitched Jacket" from *Restless Nights* by Dino Buzzati. Copyright © Dino Buzzati. **Agatha Christie**: Hughes Massie Ltd for "The Adventure of Johnnie Waverly" from *Poirot's Early Cases* by Agatha Christie, Collins 1974. Copyright © Agatha Christie 1974. **Helen Cresswell**: A. M. Heath & Co. Ltd for "The Sky Sea" by Helen Cresswell from *Hidden Turnings*, edited by Diana Wynne Jones, Methuen Children's Books 1989. Copyright © Helen Cresswell 1989. **Eleanor Farjeon**: David Higham Associates Ltd for "The Girl Who Kissed the Peach Tree" from *The Little Bookworm* by Eleanor Farjeon, Oxford University Press 1955. Copyright © Eleanor Farjeon 1955. **Ursula Le Guin**: Virginia Kidd for "Texts" by Ursula Le Guin, first appeared in *American Short Fiction* as part of the PEN Syndicated Fiction Project. Copyright © Ursula K. Le Guin 1990. **Paul Jennings**: Penguin Books Australia Ltd for "Smart Ice Cream" from *Unreal! Eight Surprising Stories* by Paul Jennings, Penguin Books Australia Ltd 1985. Copyright © Paul Jennings 1985. **Diana Wynne Jones**: Reed Consumer Books Ltd for "The Master" by Diana Wynne Jones from *Hidden Turnings*, edited by Diana Wynne Jones, Methuen Children's